EQUATION

EQUATION

HUBERT-RICHARD CLARKE

AFTERLIFE

Published by Afterlife 2024

Cover art, book design, and formatting by Hubert-Richard Clarke

Afterlife Publishers
www.equationnovel.com

ISBN: 978 1 0686515 2 6

For my devoted parents
Hubert & Dorothy

For my brothers from another mother
Alex Weir
Dan Lyman
Ron Ashford

You now walk alongside the angels on another plane, or have manifested
once again in a new form

• PROLOGUE •

It's dawn. The darkness has almost lifted. Orange and red sunrays rise to threaten the pinkish-blue sky.

Jaydon Lynch feels the grains of sand lightly scratch between his toes. He listens intently as waves crash against a craggy precipice nearby. The smell of salt permeates the air.

One could easily lose themselves in the enormity of liquid aqua—an infinite number of droplets moving in perfect unison to form the ocean's vibrational pull. Offset by a myriad of dangers veiled beneath its depths.

In his hands, he fondles a natural onyx stone necklace with an S inscribed on its surface. Jaydon glances down towards the jewellery which he holds tenderly.

The pain and the loss still cut deep, but somehow bearable. Jaydon's body remains still as his consciousness once again returns to the infinite vastness of the ocean.

THE PHONE CALL

An electric voice emanates at a distance, digitised from somewhere within this modern abode, yet to be seen. Realms of natural light disperse through the large windows of the spacious Ikea-like showroom.

This ultra-contemporary six-bedroom suburban home belongs to the Colburn family. The electric voice belongs to Marcus Webb from The Morning Show.

He delivers his daily dose of negative in an even, professional tone. 'Good morning, I'm Marcus Webb, and this is Sunrise Live at 8. Community leaders of Hatham, Pelth, and Kendersford implored government heads to reconsider their plans for a fully armed police patrol. The initiative strategy will include the eventual implementation of militarised security groups in these areas...'

The voice originates from an 85-inch screen 8K UHD TV hanging on an exposed brick kitchen wall. This is where the suited and tied Marcus's digital image sits. Small, when compared to the real-life Colburn family, as they settle into the morning routine at the kitchen table.

Mia Colburn is mostly sixteen, going on thirty-five. One of those adolescents who is continually finding spurts of maturity budding from her silliness. She is also not the awkward in her body type of teenager.

Unlike her brother, Zachary. A year younger, lanky, geeky, and self-conscious, hiding under his trendy fringe haircut.

Outside the ceiling-to-floor windows. Baxter, the families' border collie, lounges in the backyard. Streaks of sunlight break through the clouds, filtering between the gaps of the maple trees' autumn-coloured leaves, creating a pattern of light and shadow.

Caitlyn Colburn stands near the window, holding a large knife, lost in thought. The sound of the television and her children melt into the background. She stares pensively at her own reflection, a distorted closeup trapped within the silver blade. *Who are you?*

Caitlyn's part-time work as a barrister in the Crown Prosecution Service is rewarding. Her children are beautiful, almost grown. She wouldn't have it any other way. However, there remains a lingering void. She wonders *if darkness is the only thing that can fill the nagging emptiness. No, that's absurd.*

The sound of Baxter's barking draws Caitlyn out of her thoughts. She gazes upwards to see the dog chewing on a rubber toy, whilst wagging his tail. *He must be hungry.*

She views Zachary reflected through the window, emptying some dog food on a tray. Caitlyn finds a smile as Marcus continues.

He says, 'The trial is part of the radical war against crime initiative. Tensions have been steadily rising in the South West trilateral branded The Slums.

'Owing to severe unemployment, rampant drug misuse, and a steady rise in crime. The initiative begins with the rollout of an armed police patrol, closely followed by–'

Caitlyn silences the Newsman abruptly via remote control. Digital hum and black screen replace images and sounds.

She places breakfast on the table. Within each plate, the yellow of the egg's yolk breaks through the white of its poached exterior. Dribbling subtly over the gluten-free toast and smooth avocado it lies upon. Accompanied by a cashew nut and banana smoothy.

Zachary re-enters after feeding Baxter. He pulls on a wooden chair, which complains with a screech before he sits.

Benjamin Colburn will be forty-seven in a couple of days, and he looks his age. Yet, the crow's feet and greying temples seem to add an allure to his presence.

He carries himself with a powerful, fluid grace as he moves through the corridor. The tall, muscular frame fills out the shark-coloured three-piece suit tailored to a third of a millimetre. He slows to a stop and taps the speed dial on his smartphone. Then he raises the device to his ear.

Mia toys with her brother. 'No one needed to tell me anything. It's so obvious. Are you in love?'

'You're so silly sometimes, you know that.'

She reaches past Zachary to grab breakfast. He pretends to ignore her whilst texting on his iPhone. Caitlyn stands a short distance away, continuing her chores. She watches her husband intently, who is in mid-flow.

Caitlyn's ears perk up with interest in what is transpiring with her husband in the corridor. Though her children are talking, it isn't difficult to hear Benjamin, as his voice is now raised.

'Kidnapping, blackmail, grievous bodily harm with intent. Forget about a career in law. You should write fiction with an imagination like that. My client is a successful investor and a pillar of the community. If you bring us anywhere near a court of law, I will bury you.'

Benjamin ends the call with a press of a button. He looks up to find Caitlyn staring. She holds an expression that is hard to gauge.

Benjamin's wave of darkness transitions to a half smile. Caitlyn has already diverted her attention elsewhere.

'Mum, your son is in love,' Mia says.

Caitlyn is well aware of what her daughter is doing. However, she plays along with the jest. 'Is he now? What's her name?'

'How do you know it's not him?'

She looks at her son playfully. 'Well, I always had my suspicions.' They both laugh.

Benjamin's voice reaches everyone's ears before he enters the room. 'Ladies, give the guy a break.' He finds Caitlyn. Their eyes meet, and tension underscores the subsequent kiss.

He moves towards the refrigerator and opens the door. It displays a picture of an older couple, Caitlyn's parents. The family is on holiday in Japan. There are also metallic copper style fridge magnets with the notes: 'EMILY'S BIRTHDAY THIS TUESDAY. MIA TO EMPTY BINS THIS WEEK'. Then oddly, 'HI MR DAN DOLL FASE'.

Benjamin reaches deep into the recesses of the fridge. He removes some coconut milk for coffee.

Caitlyn takes a seat beside Mia. They both observe Zachary with interest. Zachary sets down his digital device. He clears his throat. 'Okay. Her name is Kazuko Himura. She's seventeen years old. We went out a few times, and we're just taking it slow. Happy?'

They fall silent for a moment, allowing the ambience of distant traffic and chirping birds to enter the fray. Then the occupants of the table suddenly burst into laughter. Zachary rolls his eyes. 'Oh, so funny.'

Mia is having a blast. 'You should see your face.' Zachary finally gives in and sees the humour, joining in with the laughter.

With a cup of coffee in one hand and some documents in the other, Benjamin draws up a chair and sits next to his son. Zachary straightens up.

'An older woman, eh? Is she pretty?'

'Yeah, she's pretty.'

'Remember to use protection, right?'

'Dad!'

'I'm just kidding.' His smile fades. 'Though I'm not.'

Caitlyn observes her husband. Drinking coffee and appraising files. Her eyes find Zachary, who has returned to the iPhone. Then, she turns her attention towards Mia, also absorbed in the latest digital device. She shakes her head in private amusement. 'Modern families.'

The landline rings. Caitlyn feels an overwhelming obligation to answer. She rises from her seat and moves towards the hallway.

Caitlyn picks up the ultra-modern cordless device and raises it to her ear. The voice on the other end feels like it is from a different plane, near supernatural.

The phone now lies on the table on its side, with the sound of the dial tone a continuous beep. *What did the voice say?* She can't remember. Nor can she hear her children speaking from the kitchen or feel their presence. She is certain that they have already departed for school. *How much time has passed?*

* * *

There were flashes of Mia as she rose from the table. Zachary, toast in hand, school bag in the other, bumped a fist with his father before he followed suit. Both of them gave her a peck on the cheek, then hurriedly made their way to the front entrance...

* * *

What happened before and after? It is hazy, off somehow, and out of sync. An overwhelming high-pitched noise is creeping up on her. The sound you hear in war and action movies as our temporarily deaf hero stops to contemplate the horrors of explosions and violence surrounding him, all in poetic slow motion.

Caitlyn has no explanation for what is happening. The emptiness has disappeared, faded away. She feels... so alive. *Everything is so vibrant.*

Benjamin Colburn glances upwards from reading his documents. Caitlyn has been missing since the phone call. 'Honey?' Nothing greets him. He listens out for a while longer. Following another moment of silence, he continues highlighting paragraphs whilst consuming his coffee.

Caitlyn makes her way through the primary bedroom, which, as with all the Colburn household, is contemporary and minimalistic.

She slides open the Japanese-style wardrobe and reaches upwards towards the top shelf. Behind a linen basket is a secured safe: steel, biometric touch ID.

She raises her hand, directing her index finger to the square where the fingerprint should go, and presses. There is a beep, followed by a click. The red light switches to green, open sesame.

If this were an artistic film helmed by a creative auteur. The view would be from within the confines of the safe. The camera capturing Caitlyn in a tight head-to-shoulder silhouette, with orchestral strings moving to a crescendo. It's very moody, atmospheric, stylish, but this is not a movie, and we're not playing make-believe.

Inside the safe is a box, and inside the box is a .22 calibre weapon. That is a gun to the uninitiated. Caitlyn lifts the magazine and adds bullets. She loads and chambers the gun, then heads downstairs.

There is weightlessness, a heightening of senses accompanied by vibrant technicolour. *Maybe this is the spiritual enlightenment gurus philosophise about.*

She holds the Gun in one hand whilst her fingers graze lightly against the wall with the other as if appreciating touch for the first time. She moves along the corridor.

A gun click gains Benjamin's attention, forcing him to look up and away from his work. Caitlyn stands in the hallway. She points the weapon in his direction.

Benjamin sits frozen, a bewildered expression on his face. He then slowly ascends. Hands raised, fear in his eyes.

Caitlyn can see that her husband is desperately trying to reason. However, his words are inaudible, drowned out by the high-pitched ringing that has now intensified into white light. Then... Everything fades away, leaving her in deafening silence, as Benjamin mouths the words. 'Caitlyn, please don't.'

Their eyes meet, and tension underscores the subsequent kill. Caitlyn pulls the trigger. The gunshot breaks the silence.

• 2 •

TWO LIONS AND A CROWN

The city ambience from below melds into the scattering of diffused sunlight and seeps into a second-floor studio apartment's open window. Though, it's as if a majority of the exterior's luminance has stopped short of this room, just out of reach.

An alarm clock sits on the bedside table, within the confines of the minimalist abode, guttering laid bare to see. The clock reads *13.15* in a whitish-blue hue. Central colon flashing between the numbers, alight in digital buzz.

The bed is untouched, neat, and immaculate. If anyone lives here, they have not slept in this spot for days.

Away from the untouched bed is the living room area, bathroom, and kitchen, which are all open-plan. The place is sparse. That's why the ocean turquoise coloured acoustic guitar sitting in a corner is noticeable.

Jaydon Lynch lies on the sofa before a modern glass table. He is half asleep, dressed scruffily in a dark t-shirt and loose, dark cotton trousers. He stirs, then rises groggily from his stupor to a weary stretch, finding a sitting position.

His laptop and an abundance of police files lay next to a digital newspaper device. Amongst the files lies a black leather ID wallet with a silver crested emblem—a crown hovers over a shield, with a lion on either side. The words, 'DETECTIVE CHIEF INSPECTOR', accompany the two magnificent creatures standing on hind legs. Jaydon is a cop.

A scattering of white pills lay next to an open bottle with the label, 'Paroxetine'. A few half-empty cups of black coffee sit alongside last night's leftovers.

The newspaper digital device includes a patchwork of several headlines and articles, such as, 'Another Doll, Another Victim', and 'Calculating Killer Eludes Capture'. They share space with 'Missing Girl Reunites with Family After 15 years'.

Jaydon's eyes skim a missing person's report, with details such as, 'height: 5 feet, weight: 105lbs, eye colour: hazel, sex: female, age: 15 years'. His attention is now diverted to a blue origami unicorn lying next to the computer screen.

He lifts the origami tenderly for closer inspection. Upon doing so, the hairs raise on the back of his neck. Jaydon turns towards the feeling, but it is just an empty room. *I need to get some sleep.*

Jaydon gazes at the origami fondly, reminiscing. There is a figure that his eyes discern in the near distance, a young girl, in her mid-teens, with dark brown hair and hazel eyes. She wears casual blue denim and a purple jersey. She seems to have materialised from nowhere.

The girl smiles. He somehow catches a breath. Right now, at this moment, they are the only two people in the universe. Jaydon outstretches his arm, offering a hand for the girl to take.

The jangling of his mobile phone breaks the moment. He glances downwards at the device. Along with six missed calls is a text message, which reads, 'I need you here,' followed by an uptown suburb address. His gaze returns upwards. No one is there. Jaydon rubs his face tiredly, then exhales deeply.

Jaydon opens the bathroom cabinet and scans the toiletries, which have an array of prescription drugs on display. This includes, 'Fluoxetine', and 'Valium'. Before recently, Jaydon had never given a second thought to taking prescribed medicine in all of his forty-three years of life.

He reaches for the legal drugs and closes the cabinet shut, forced to meet his reflection in its mirror—a stranger holding a thousand-yard stare.

His brown curly hair contains a whisper of grey glimmer, and his face looks surprisingly young for his years, with expressive cheekbones. His dark brown eyes convey pain through his intense glare, yet are oddly trusting and at odds with the two-inch vertical scar that cuts from eyebrow to cheek.

He embarks upon a momentary examination of the soul. There is an emptiness that lies with open arms, waiting patiently for the darkness to let herself in.

He moves away from the cabinet, pours the drugs down the toilet, and then flushes. The pills disappear into the swirling abyss of water, pipes, and the sound of Bhu-Woosh!

Jaydon has now taken a shower and shaved, clothed in a black top and slim trousers. He stands directly above the table. A warped reflection in the glass, attention aimed towards the assortment of police files and newspaper digital device.

Jaydon's eyes find the leather police ID. There is an intense charge, a change in his persona. He scoops up the badge and moves to the closet.

He reaches for his dark brown leather jacket, which is loosely placed on the clothes hanger. Before closing the closet, he notices the tan-coloured, open-faced, retro-modern motorcycle helmet that lies on its side. *It's been a while.* Jaydon hesitates for a moment before retrieving the helmet.

Riding a motorcycle has always captivated Jaydon. There is a heightening of the senses. You see and feel all. It's IMAX on steroids. Once the combination of fear, exhilaration, relaxation, and pleasure combines, the mind disappears, and everything becomes one. This is the way of Zen.

Jaydon's Zero DSR Electric Motorbike sounds like something from the film Tron. He hurtles along the city street towards the scene of the crime.

• 3 •

A TALE OF TWO NEIGHBOURHOODS

Detective Jaydon Lynch's motorbike slows to a stop outside of the crime scene. Police vehicles, paramedics, and flashing lights surround the Colburn residence, whilst blue and white crime tape keeps the ever-growing crowd and news reporters at bay.

The city's finest question the locals, who loiter outside their houses, looking on in concern and despair. A crime like this is extremely rare in this neck of the woods.

Now, if this were The Slums, it would be a different story. In fact, it wouldn't be that much of a story. Jaydon knows this too well, as he spent the formative years of his life in Pelth, the worst of The Slums.

*. *. *.

It was just him and his mother, Frederica. His father, Lamont, left them to fend for themselves when he was eight years of age. Frederica tried the best she could, whilst delirium ensued around them. Cracks appeared within the protective wall this woman had built, seeping into their existence.

Crimes were up tenfold. The Slums were in chaos. Criminals ran rampant on the streets. The Municipal Police, under extreme pressure and woefully undertrained, shot and paralysed a woman named Marie Stephenson in her own home. They were searching for her son, Michael, a known felon. This was to ignite the third 'Slum Riots'.

Jaydon vividly remembers a specific night during the revolt in which a disgruntled mob launched a firebomb through the window of a nearby corner shop. With the flames ablaze, the police lost control of the vandalised streets as the looters ran havoc.

Frederica stood silent. She gazed with sad eyes at the madness taking place outside of her bedroom window. Jaydon was at his mother's side, trying to gauge her thoughts. Though the look in her eyes hindered him from joining in with the activities that same night.

When Jaydon awoke the next day, the teenager drifted tiredly downstairs and discovered a packed suitcase. Frederica sat at the living room table. She had her mind made up. He was going to live with his grandparents, Joseph and Gertrude.

Jaydon surveys the scene up ahead. He watches and waits a while longer.

• 4 •

ANATOMY OF A CRIME

A police radio crackles from within the building. Cameras snap sporadically, causing flashes of light to break through the malaise. Like ghosts, the CSI's, wearing white overalls from head to toe, drift around the Colburn residence. Quite fitting, as the airy modern space currently feels like a mausoleum.

They painstakingly scrutinise every corner. Cataloguing data through videos and pictures, collecting fingerprints, gunshot residue, hair fibres, scraping dried blood, and so forth.

This is not a glamorous job, and they are not the crime solvers portrayed on TV. The work is a tedious mixture of science, logic, and assisting the law.

Detective Superintendent Gavin Reece rolls the bronze sobriety coin over the back of his knuckles into his palm and then returns the gesture in a continuous motion. The fifty-seven-year-olds thoughts pass to Jaydon with a wave of emotions. *I should have done more.*

He scans the surrounding scene, and for a moment wonders, *what made these people choose this work?* For him, it's simple. It is a part of his very being. Gavin is real police through and through. Though here, he still feels like an outsider.

✳ ✳ ✳

Originally from Baltimore, USA, he policed as a tough patrolman in an even tougher neighbourhood. Then Evelyn came along—a schoolteacher from England who had been working on a cultural exchange program for a year.

She arrived in the States single, and was married when it was time for her return to the UK. He soon followed. That was twenty-five years ago.

✳ ✳ ✳

Jaydon crawls to a stop near the blue and white police tape. Patrolman Wilson approaches, intending to move him along. Jaydon removes his helmet, face scarf and protective goggles. Then, he shows the officer his phone messages and badge. 'I have received an invitation.' Wilson recognises Detective Lynch. He relinquishes and lets him through.

Jaydon parks up his bike and bows under the tape. He moves towards the Colburn home, mind already in detective mode.

Jaydon can't help but feel slightly self-conscious as he conducts an initial walk through the crime scene. There are medics, a forensic pathologist in the distance, CSI's, and the police, who offer head turns and subtle glances. Yet his instincts kick in. Eyes searching for clues, anything unusual.

A forensic dust for prints on the landline phone. Do people still have those outside the office? He observes closer, noticing no wiring. It is a VOIP. *That makes more sense.*

Gavin moves in his direction, offering a hand, which Jaydon takes. 'The prodigal son.' Jaydon and Gavin are as close as two work colleagues can be without knowing everything about each other's lives outside of the job.

He has met Evelyn several times, a smart lady who instantly makes you feel comfortable. 'I'm glad you're here, Jaydon.'

Gavin is an above-average-height man with a lived-in face, great instincts, and a sharp mind. There is an internal intensity permeating through his toned, wiry frame. His demeanour is that of a street-smart intellectual, an old-school tough guy, and a yogi. 'How are you keeping?'

To be truthful, Jaydon is not sure how to answer that question. This all feels a little surreal, being back on a crime scene. He scans the room, taking it all in. Jaydon eyes Gavin for a short while, measuring him. 'What is this, Gavin?'

Gavin glances over at the wall on the other side of the room. This catches Jaydon's attention as well.

'Just the other day, they arrested a fifteen-year-old boy for raping and killing his teacher. He didn't like that she called him out for misbehaving in class.'

'I read about it.'

'Did you read about the firearms initiative they're deploying downtown? Arming us to the teeth, and that's just the beginning. It's a bad idea.'

'It may well be.'

'Berg would be glad to see you out and about.'

'Is he working on this case?'

'A double homicide in Hatham.'

Jaydon scans the area. *I'm not sure if I'm ready.*

Gavin appraises Jaydon for a moment. 'Let's just walk the scene.' Radio static and murmuring cops lurking in corners fill out the tension in the air.

The VOIP phone device diverts Jaydon's attention. He moves towards the CSI, dusting for prints. He is careful not to touch the evidence or disturb her. The first thing he notices is the time the receiver has been idle, which is close to 240 minutes. The battery is near dead.

Upon returning to the kitchen, Jaydon and Gavin find their attention once again diverted by the writing on the wall. They let it simmer and approach the main area of the crime.

Mike, the forensic pathologist, briefly glances upwards from his work. He then continues to finish his examination of Mr Colburn, who is now deceased. 'DCI Lynch, meet Benjamin Colburn.'

Benjamin Colburn lays stiff, his dead eyes wide open, staring into space. The blood that once protruded from the bullet wounds was now a dry red, covering his clothing. A nearby CSI takes photos. Snap! Followed by a white flash.

Jaydon moves towards the dead man. The Crime Scene Investigator hands him a pair of nitrile gloves, which he slips on. He kneels to examine more closely. 'Judging from pupil dilation, body temperature, and the status of rigour mortis. I'd say the victim has been deceased for approximately four hours.'

Mike offers a nod of professional acknowledgement to Jaydon. 'That's correct.'

Gavin chimes in. 'It also lines up with the neighbours who called it in.'

Jaydon calculates that the minutes on the idle phone and the time of death seem to coincide. His eyes scan the body and attire. A couple of extravagant rings remain on Benjamin's fingers. His clothes are not unkempt, and the flow of blood doesn't defy gravity. *Nobody tampered with the victim postmortem.*

His eidetic brain recites each entry point with which he has come into contact. No forced entry. *This wasn't a home robbery.* Jaydon concludes that from the trajectory of the bullet, the shooter calmly stood in the corridor a few feet away and pulled the trigger. But this wasn't an execution. *He knew the assailant.* 'His wife?'

Gavin nods. 'The first officers who arrived found her sitting there.' He motions to an empty chair in the corner. 'Bright-eyed, but no recollection.'

'Drugs?'

'No drugs in her system,' Mike says. He and the CSI wrap Benjamin in a white cloth. They will then place paper bags over his hands and feet for transportation to the morgue. 'We'll confirm C.O.D post-mortem. Though I'd say it looks fairly obvious.'

Gavin takes over. 'Her prints are all over the murder weapon. She has no memory of what transpired. It's all gone blank. At least that's what she says.'

'Psych evaluation?'

'As we speak.'

Jaydon stands. *Why am I here?* He recalibrates and then focuses his attention on the nearby wall, which he moves towards with purpose.

'Years ago, one of my first cases. There was a man who killed his entire family. When we arrived on the scene, he was just standing there, bug-eyed.' Gavin gazes out of the window for a moment. He seems to be deep in thought.

He moves towards Jaydon and continues. 'Contrary to the evidence, he always maintained his innocence, claiming it was somebody else's doing. He died in prison, never changing his statement. Something always bothered me about that case. The thing is, his penmanship is eerily similar to Mrs Colburn's.'

Jaydon becomes transfixed. He is now standing directly in front of this mystery, fully engaged.

Gavin is not far behind. 'Jaydon, I need to be sure that this is just the act of a crazy woman and nothing more.'

Written on the wall is a mathematical formula. Circles within circles, making patterns of symbols and numbers done in demented repetition. A CSI points their camera in this direction—a snap followed by a white flash.

INTO THE ABYSS

Formally known as White Lake Police Station, The King's Court Special Branch is home to the Major Crimes Command and several other specialist territorial police groups. Four buildings have housed the country's finest since the nineteenth century.

When the science of forensics and detective work was in its infancy, small rural police forces with limited experience would be out of their depth if a witness-less murder took place. They would require help from The King's Court.

Most of the country's modern police forces have sufficiently trained forensic technicians and specialised staff. So, this branch is no longer obligated to help with homicide-related cases outside of this conurbation.

Yet, they aid The National Crime Agency with counter-terrorism, fraud, ballistics, and large-scale complex criminal investigations. The King's Court also offers its resources nationally for high-profile cases, such as serial murders.

This building is a refurbished marriage of a contemporary interior and neoclassical shell, confined within its seven storeys of open-plan office space. Plain-clothed police sit at desks, working on laptops and digital devices. The humongous windows of the top floor showcase this megalopolis's skyline.

* * *

Deep down in the basement recesses of this building, there is a sparsely furnished interview room. A large glass one-way mirror partially fills one side, offering a haunted reflection of Jaydon and Caitlyn Colburn, who sit facing each other in the well-lit area. A metal desk decorated with files and a couple of manila folders parts them.

* * *

Gavin stands in the confines of the darkened adjoining room. He bears witness through the one-way glass.

Advisor to the deputy mayor of police and crime and CPS prosecutor, Dominic Remel, enters hurriedly. He loosens his shirt collar and then throws a dark brown leather briefcase onto a nearby table with a thud. 'So, she shot him?'

Gavin glances at Dominic before returning his attention to what is about to transpire in the other room. 'Yes, it looks like it. What are you doing here?'

'This is a high-profile case, and my superiors have taken an interest. Anything else is beyond our pay grades.'

Gavin takes a breath and offers no quarrel. He knows when to let sleeping dogs lie. On this one, *just do the job the best you can.* 'Caitlyn Xylia Colburn. No priors. No history of mental illness or drug abuse. It appears she just snapped.'

'What evidence do you have?'

'Pathology report, trace samples, DNA. It's solid. Plus, her fingerprints were all over the weapon.'

Gavin reluctantly hands over the preliminary findings to Dominic, who scans through the pages with interest. 'Pretty open and shut, it seems.'

Gavin observes Jaydon and Caitlyn on the other side. His thoughts return to Malcom Reiss. The man who killed his whole family all those years ago. *That incident was also open and shut.* Yet something always troubled him about it. Like a recurring splinter in his mind. 'I guess we're all capable of the unthinkable.'

Dominic stops reading and takes a mental note. 'Yes, you, me, Mr Jones, from across the street. Your detectives, who continue to stare into the abyss.'

Gavin ponders for a moment. 'Just about long enough for it to stare back.'

Jaydon appraises Caitlyn. He then slides one of the brown manila folders in her direction. Their eyes lock for a moment.

A hesitant Caitlyn now glances down towards the folder, which she opens with some trepidation. Photos of a deceased Benjamin are on display. She is transported back to that moment...

*　*　*

Caitlyn stood in the hallway. The cool metal gun in her grasp. Her heightened gaze fixed on a terrified Benjamin.

She held her breath and pointed the gun whilst her fingers caressed the trigger. There was a split second of hesitation before...

*　*　*

'Mrs Colburn, are you still with me?'

Caitlyn returns from her horrific recollection. She slams the folder shut and slides it across the desk, back towards Jaydon with a slight tremor. She then briskly pulls away.

Caitlyn is still trying to figure it out. She remembers what transpired, though she does not know why. *This can't be happening.* Just for an instant, this morning was... and then... Caitlyn feels nothing but pain, loss, and despair.

Jaydon appraises her intently. Following a pause, he opens a folder with a collection of photos displaying the enigmatic mathematical formula. He turns the folder 180 degrees clockwise and slides it towards her purview.

This triggers her instantly as she glares at the images contained within. 'There was a voice,' Caitlyn whispers.

'Voice? The person you spoke with on the phone this morning. Is that who you mean? Were they a part of this?'

Caitlyn stares at the photographs, transfixed. There is almost a hypnotic quality to the sequence of numbers that draws her in. It brings her back once more...

On the wall was the equation, written in red. The gun remained in her possession, along with a felt-tip marker. She found her dead husband lying a few feet away. This horrified Caitlyn. She dropped both items instantly and staggered backwards from the dead man.

Caitlyn scanned her surroundings for some sort of explanation. There was none. Only an empty chair, which she collapsed into in a state of shock. Wailing police sirens drew near, whilst Baxter, fuelled by fear, barked aggressively in the backyard.

Caitlyn Colburn glances upwards from the images and holds Jaydon's gaze with trepidation in her eyes. She feels the vacuous pull. 'Detective Lynch. Do you sometimes feel a void that only darkness can fill?'

Jaydon momentarily pauses. Then he raises his fingers to his mouth with a slight tremor.

Caitlyn perceives the voice in her mind playing like a broken record, although muffled and echoed. This, combined with the room's overhead lights, makes her dizzy.

'He started this, and he is going to finish it.'

'Excuse me?'

Unsteady and lightheaded, Caitlyn rises from her chair. It feels like the walls are closing in. Jaydon also ascends from his seat.

'You're not prepared for what's coming,' Caitlyn says as she backs away and shrinks into a corner. Her eyes are mad and wide with panic.

Jaydon moves towards her and slowly lowers to reassure. Caitlyn tightly grabs hold of his arm, like a drowning person trying to stay afloat. He lightly cups her face. 'Breathe.'

Caitlyn does as he says, gaining some composure. Jaydon checks his watch. He glances upwards towards the one-way mirror. 'I'm ending this interview.'

RULE OF LAW

Lyle Fletcher is not a flashy type of guy, but he is a brilliant lawyer. Some would say one of the best. For Lyle, there's no magic pill for success; it's just a formula. Work harder for longer than everybody else, research, prepare, and never overlook the small stuff.

The one thing he was not prepared for was the notification he received on his phone this afternoon. Now, here he is, sitting with Caitlyn in an interrogation room, acting as her defence council. *This makes no sense.*

Both he and Caitlyn went to law school together. He knows her well. There was never misuse of drugs, signs of violence, aggression, or impulsive behaviour. At least based on what he was aware of. *Just remember, your job is to provide a thorough defence.*

'Jesus, Caitlyn, what were you thinking speaking to the police without representation?'

Caitlyn stares into space and mutters under her breath. 'I don't know. I just thought that...'

He observes her with concern. *We need another psych evaluation.* 'You're not a flight risk and a model citizen. Bail should be possible, but from now on, you stay silent whilst we prepare your defence.' She nods solemnly.

Caitlyn is in her early forties with shoulder-length black hair, presently tied loosely into a ponytail. Her brown skin is even and smooth. She has intense, unusual features, with something bubbling below the surface. *She's still a beautiful woman*, he thinks.

*. *. *.

Jaydon stands deep in thought alongside Gavin and Dominic. He observes Caitlyn through the looking glass, who is receiving legal advice from her council. Visuals, but no sound, courtesy of a microphone on mute. As is their right via the rule of law.

Jaydon knows evil. He has faced it many times. He is also aware that seemingly regular people are capable of the heinous. Yet, Caitlyn Colburn is not giving him that vibe.

'What was that?' Dominic asks, breaking the silence.

'I don't understand what you mean,' Gavin says.

Dominic stands a little taller. 'What I mean is that your guy is a police officer, not a councillor. With the act she just pulled, it's my guess they'll plead not guilty through temporary insanity at the arraignment.'

'Were photos of her murdered husband not hardball enough for you? The goal of the interrogator is to elicit information, not push the accused into a corner.'

'Yet, that's literally what happened.'

Gavin calmly looks Dominic square in the eyes. 'Don't test me.'

Jaydon continues to stare long and hard towards the occupants on the other side of the glass. Caitlyn's words echo through his mind. *Do you sometimes feel a void that only darkness can fill? Why did she ask that?*

Dominic backs down somewhat, returning his attention to the accused and her defence. 'Ironic, isn't it?'

'How so?'

'Her husband would have been the best defence for her now.'

Jaydon chimes in. 'It wasn't an act.'

'You think someone else was involved?' Gavin asks.

'She kept mentioning some kind of voice. I can't explain this, but something transpired during that call.'

'Our technicians conducted a trace. It was a burner. We got nothing. Maybe they destroyed the phone after use.'

'What are you implying?' Dominic asks.

'I'm not sure what I'm implying. I just feel we need to dig a little deeper.'

'May I speak freely?'

'Knock yourself out.'

'I don't believe Detective Lynch should be here. He's not ready.'

Gavin mulls over Dominic's opinion and then appraises Jaydon with concern. He then takes Jaydon by the elbow and steers him into a corner. They speak in hushed tones. 'Jaydon–'

'I'm fine.'

'You know, Hobbes and Rousseau are still out there, chasing leads.'

'I'm fine. You called me, remember?'

Gavin absorbs this for a moment. He then turns to Dominic. 'My Detective stays.'

• 7 •

HAROLD, THE GIANT KILLER

Viatex Inc. is a company in love with its own lies. There are digital adverts on MAC-type flat screens, with slogans like 'Viatex Inc, creating a better future for all.' Showcasing perfect families, flashing unnaturally white teeth, whilst the spotless white corridors, clean line aesthetics, and the uneasy stillness wouldn't be out of place in an isolationist Sci-Fi novel.

Head scientist Harold Mansfield sits at his office desk, phone in hand. The heart-aching strings of Bach's Cello Suite No.1 G Major float from the ultra-modern music system stationed in the room's corner.

He raises the phone close to his ear. A voice speaks at the other end of the line.

'Harold Mansfield?' says the voice.

'Yes.'

'Harold Edward Mansfield?'

A sense of calmness overcomes Harold.

'This is he.'

'A = 1 or 0, Em = 1 or 4, kill or die, make your choice.'

The beginnings of a high-pitch ring emerge. The voice is no more.

✳. ✳. ✳.

Raindrops spatter the street in an atmospheric clatter. Distant city lights form illuminating shapes upon the black of night. In proximity, street lamps and a display of interior lights from a row of houses create reflections on the sheen of the wet road. The far-off urban ambience provides a subdued soundtrack within the hazy mist.

We locate Jaydon, who sits on his Zero DSR Electric Motorbike. He observes a nearby apartment building.

A light brightens the room on the top floor of the two-story townhouse. This grabs Jaydon's attention. The figure of a dark-haired woman drifts towards the window as if sensing his presence.

Jaydon feels the energy of her gaze whilst his heart throbs against his chest. He removes his helmet. *Are these tears on my face, or is it the rain?*

The figure outstretches an arm, finding a switch. The room dims. She backs away and out of sight.

Jaydon returns his helmet and buckles the chin strap. He then rides away, disappearing into the night.

Harold can't explain it. The genius of Bach continues to provide him company, but it's different. He can feel the vibrancy of the strings in vivid detail, like it is a part of him. Time has skipped. The music has progressed further along.

The phone receiver lies on his desk, dial tone at the ready. He occasionally glimpses towards his laboratory next door through the office's large off-blue glass window.

On his desk is a digital newspaper device, which he scans through. It contains headlines such as, 'Arthritis Drug Coxifam Withdrawn from Shelves After Deadly Side Effects'. One article has a picture of Viatex Inc. CEO Robert Richardson, Harold's boss.

He opens his desk drawer and retrieves a report. His eyes skim the words, '...strongly linked to heart disease and strokes.' '...possibly up to five hundred thousand people affected.' *No six-dollar salary or NDA will keep me quiet any longer. The truth is light, and I will be the torchbearer.*

Harold has just completed etching something onto his desk with a sharp instrument. He presses his telephone intercom, which buzzes momentarily before someone picks up with a click. The voice at the other end is strong and confident, a man of power. 'Yes.'

'May I have a word with you?'

Robert offers a sigh. 'Come on up, Harold.'

Harold calmly replaces the handset. It is hard to verbalise what he's feeling. *Some kind of euphoria?*

* * *

The beam of an overhead lamp hones over Jaydon's shoulder in the dimly lit room. He is crouched on the wooden floor, cross-legged. Police files and forensic photos of the Colburn crime scene surround him. There is also a report on the homicide that Gavin mentioned.

* * *

Malcom Reiss was a forty-nine-year-old engineer who killed his wife and son. There was nothing unusual in this man's profile: no mental illness, history of violence, or addictions. The neighbours found him to be mild-mannered and insightful.

His wife, Lyndsay, was a youth worker. His teenage son, Scott, was a college student studying English Literature.

Forensic evidence concluded Malcolm strangled Lyndsay. It appears Scott returned home and interrupted him during the process. Malcolm must have pushed or elbowed Scott out of the way, who stumbled and hit his head against the corner of a nearby table. He died instantly.

The last thing Malcolm could remember that afternoon was speaking to a visitor at his office. Then, what followed was a vast gap in his memory.

He regained consciousness and found himself at home, surrounded by his dead family and a mathematical equation written on the wall in his hand.

* * *

A car alarm, and the distant wail of a police siren, offer some ambience to Jaydon's silent apartment. He views some black-and-white forensic images. It's Benjamin Colburn. The dead man posed, almost artistic in a twisted sense.

Jaydon mentally notes some of Caitlyn's initial statements. Quotes such as, *'I've never touched a gun in my life,'* pique his interest.

Jaydon finds the mysterious mathematical symbols written on the wall. Then another image grabs his attention. In the distance are words on a refrigerator.

* * *

Harold moves purposefully down the tenth-floor corridor of Viatex Inc. He passes a cleaner conducting chores, who offers Harold a nod and little else.

Harold approaches a glass lift and enters after following the usual procedure of pressing buttons and waiting. The doors close with a ding. The lift flies skyward.

Robert Richardson stands behind his desk, viewing the city through the large office window. His reflection swims between plates of glass. He admires the immense view of night lights laid out like carpet at his feet.

He doesn't turn to address Harold, who has now entered after knocking. 'Make it quick. I'm meeting my wife for dinner in an hour.'

Harold stands ominously silent in the doorway, his eyes never leaving Robert. He closes the door behind him and moves towards his boss.

Robert turns and begins speaking, but Harold can't hear him. The intense, high-pitched ring muffles the voice. Then there is silence. A blissful silence that crescendos into an emanating white light.

* * *

Back on the tenth floor, the cleaner has little time for night lights and vistas. He is too busy, working away with one of those silent vacuums, his ears encased in headphones, surrounding him with blissful modern Jazz.

However, he finds time for what comes next, which is the one-second view of Harold Mansfield and Robert Richardson forming circles in mid-air as they plummet downwards towards the ground. The startled cleaner quickly removes his headphones.

There are screams and then murmuring of stunned nearby bystanders down below. The cleaner cautiously moves towards the window that lays bare this darkly tragic comedy.

He morbidly investigates to find the CEO and disgruntled employee. Their bodies lay broken on top of a severely damaged Porsche. The car's flashing lights and wailing alarm protest in unison. His visage is that of terror and utter shock. The cleaner moves away and out of sight.

8

A FALL FROM DISGRACE

The average distance at which the earth orbits the sun is 584million miles. The duration of a complete orbit is 365.256 days, covering 1.6million miles per day.

Within each of these days, as with trillions before, the glowing sphere of hydrogen, helium, carbon, and nitrogen, which the earth revolves around, whilst rotating on its axis, sheds light on what occurred the previous night.

It is now 8 o'clock in the morning. Viatex Inc. is currently closed. Not open for business, ladies and gentlemen.

A troubled Gavin sits in Harold's office. The CSI's have all but completed their work on the top floor, whilst the clean-up crew, CSI's, and forensic pathologist have cleared the street below. *A fall from disgrace.*

He continues to read one of many files left neatly on Harold's desk. There is a plethora of documents that provide detailed information.

Certain words within sentences draw Gavin's attention: '...bribery of pharmacists and doctors,' '...unreported side effects,' '...submitting false claims to the government.' *All in service to the mighty profit.*

Gavin removes his reading glasses and places them on the table. He rubs his eyes, then takes a sip of coffee, momentarily glancing at the dark liquid, a delivery device for caffeine.

He tries to recall when all these confusing names began. Capuchino, Late, Espresso, Affogato. *What the hell, man! Black, and keep it coming.*

Is this a Western problem or a modern one? Too much choice, born from excessive ease, comfort, and little adversary. *At least for some.*

Gavin replaces his glasses. His attention diverts to a memo written by Harold. He senses Jaydon but doesn't look up. Instead, Gavin greets him by reading aloud. "We are a walking disease that forever spreads. Profiting through lies and deceit whilst poisoning thousands. Why should we care when there are billions to be made?"

Gavin stops and glances upwards to find Jaydon, who seems a little less on edge. He also appears to be a man who has finally experienced some sleep.

'A memo from Harold Mansfield, Chief Analytical Scientist to Robert Richardson, Vice CEO of Viatex Inc. And it goes on. So, I will quote. 'The longer I work here, the more I feel I have sold my soul to the devil.' End quote. This man may have an impressive array of letters after his name, but grammar is not his strong suit.'

Gavin hands the memo over to Jaydon, who skims the document with interest. However, Jaydon is more concerned with what is on Harold's desk. The same mathematical formula, clearly visible in plain sight, engraved into the desk's oak.

'It was the first thing I noticed,' Gavin says.

Jaydon moves towards the phone. Gavin stops him in his tracks. 'Don't bother; the call is untraceable.'

Jaydon turns and leaves the room. He moves away with purpose and focus.

'Where are you going?'

9

WHAT IS THE EQUATION?

Jaydon stands on one side of a glass board. Symbols and pieces of maths formula partially obscure his face.

He glances towards the large open window of The White Lake's top floor and views the metropolitan consortium. Jaydon observes the office space with all the trimmings and glass ceiling. He absorbs the ambience of the nation's finest working cases and catches wind of a junior detective through the window of the adjacent office. The young man is fresh-faced and appears eager. *I was once that way...*

Two local men found a body washed up on the river-side. A female with no identification, trace evidence, or matches in the local database for missing persons.

This was one of Jaydon's first homicide cases as a detective inspector. With the biological profile completed, he worked painstakingly with the International Commission of Missing Persons. They finally generated a match.

The young woman's name was Jiayi Ho, a twenty-one-year-old illegal Chinese immigrant from the coastal province of Fujian. She left her family for the chance of a better life, being poor and with few options. The naïve often fall victim to the criminals' deception and abuse.

The tattoo on her neck tracked her back to Wǒ-Fú-Wù—a major Triad gang that forced her into prostitution. Jaydon infiltrated the operation and masqueraded as a customer. He gained the trust of several young women in the Triad's clutches and gathered proof. Once they accumulated sufficient evidence, the police raided the gang's locations.

The captives were young, a few in their late teens. Some had cigarette burns and bruises on them. On others, there was much worse. The Major Command rescued twenty-three young women in total.

They rounded up low-level Wǒ-Fú-Wù in the raids but had nothing on the mid-level boss, Jaw-Long Tseng. A legitimate business portfolio and slick veneer shielded the Triad lieutenant. Jaydon knew that Jaw-Long Tseng 'Red Pole' frequented The Emerald Dynasty restaurant every Friday evening.

He was told implicitly by his superiors to: 'Keep a distance.' Sugar-coated with, 'Be happy with what you have.' 'We got a win.' Jaw-Long was what they called a bank, meaning in with the right people and untouchable for the time being.

As he entered the crowded establishment, Jaydon clocked at least five Triad members stationed in near proximity to Jaw-Long, who sat alone, enjoying his meal.

Though aware, he barely offered Jaydon a glance as he approached. His men perked up and moved towards the detective. Jaw-Long nonchalantly raised a hand. They eased away.

Jaydon took a seat facing the Red Pole whilst his heart raced. He eye-balled the man for a moment before he spoke. 'We know who you are.'

Jaw-Long stopped eating and gazed upwards. He straightened up and raised a napkin to his mouth with a natural grace and poise. His voice was calm, melodic. 'Really? Who is that?'

'A criminal, a lowlife, and a thug dressed in an Armani suit.'

Jaw-Long had collar-length, long hair and a slim build, with high cheekbones and immaculately smooth, unblemished skin. He had an ethereal countenance. Yet, beneath the angelic-like exterior, one could feel something dark, twisted, and truly sinister, ready to manifest.

'No, Detective Lynch. I am a legitimate businessman.'

'Not everybody's afraid of you,' Jaydon said as he trembled slightly.

'Well, they should be.'

Maybe it was the fact that Jaydon had nothing, and he knew Jaw-Long was cognisant of this. Maybe it was his tiredness or the recollection of those abused women. The visuals were still fresh in his mind. He snapped.

Jaydon made a beeline for the Triad leader and offered a beat-down as a stunned crowd gasped at what they were witnessing. Jaw-Long's men moved in, yanked Jaydon away from the Red Pole, and quickly surrounded him. Jaydon made swift work of two of them before the others overpowered him.

The Triad boss recomposed himself, hardly flustered. Jaydon, down on the floor and being beaten, took the legs out from one of the men who punched and kicked him. Dragging the thug down to the ground.

He then removed his gun from its holster before things got any worse. The 49'ers and Blue Lanterns eased off, made their distance, and then straightened their well-tailored suits over tattooed bodies.

A bruised Jaydon raised up and backed away towards the entrance. 'Give me a reason.' His gun pointed in their direction. His finger itched on the trigger. 'You make a mistake...' Jaw-Long just offered a smile. As he never did. Jaydon exited the door and moved out of sight.

One person who received justice was Jiayi following the arrest of the perpetrator. Local investor Nelson Wraith faced successful prosecution for her murder, in which DI Lynch played a prominent role.

Several years later, through hard work and the occasional annoyance to his superiors, Jaydon moved up the ranks to detective chief inspector.

*. *. *.

Jaydon turns his attention to Gavin, who has now entered the room. He points to the glass board with his felt-tip pen. 'Two murders, one suicide, eight terms?'

'Terms?'

Jaydon singles out a selection of carefully written maths symbols with the tip of his marker. 'Terms usually contain numerals.' He underlines a 0.

'Or variables, which is a letter used for an unknown. They connect through a chain to form an expression.' Jaydon underlines a whole mathematical sentence.

'I knew that,' Gavin says playfully.

'This expression contains symbols I have never seen before. If I were to hazard a guess, I would say they have a hidden meaning.' Jaydon places the marker on a nearby table. 'This is just the beginning.'

'Not if I have anything to do with it.'

Their eyes locate the voice tinged with local dialect. DCI Berg has entered the room. He views the mathematical scrawl. 'Pretty impressive. All this from memory?'

'Crime lab photos.'

'Did you need them?'

Jaydon can't quite find the half-smile he deserves. They shake hands. 'I meant to keep in touch,' Jaydon says.

Berg is thirty-eight years old, with a medium build on an athletic frame. A cop is not what you would picture at first glance. He has short-cropped black hair, tanned skin, and piercing light brown-coloured eyes.

You could see this man as a personal trainer or on a football field. One of those players at an international tournament whose team always seems to have more luck than your own.

'Jaydon, you don't have to explain anything to me. Not an iota. What you've been through. I never would have given up, you know that.'

Jaydon nods. He knows Berg understands pain. When he was just fifteen years old, someone murdered his twin sister, Amelia.

'Your pain. People understand, but they don't know. I do.'

'What happened to your sister was a tragedy,' Gavin says.

Berg smiles sadly. 'Fifteen years old. I suppose that's why I became a police officer. To find justice for the other Amelia's out there.'

'How's the case? Any leads?' Jaydon asks.

'No witnesses, no evidence, no help. We're doing our best. Life in The Slums is a little below cheap. That being said, Chief, I can still help with this.'

Gavin considers. 'Fine, but the double homicide in Hatham takes priority.'

Berg nods. He turns to Jaydon and taps him on the shoulder. 'Anything you need.'

'Sure thing.'

Berg walks away.

Gavin appraises Jaydon with measured concern, as he gazes off darkly into the distance.

• 10 •

STORY OF THE NIGHT

A knife slices through red and black police tape that reads, 'CRIME SCENE DO NOT CROSS'. It's the golden hour.

Jaydon Lynch stands silhouetted against the dying beams of a mauve and orange sunset. The large open windows of the Colburn residence frame the real-life picture in motion. A detective retreading the scene of the crime.

Jaydon slowly makes his way through the vestiges of what once seemed a happy home. His thoughts remain with Caitlyn. *Do you sometimes feel a void that only darkness can fill?*

He drifts past Colburn family members upon white walls. They hold immortalised smiles confined within frameless contemporary photographs.

He arrives at the location of Benjamin's murder. She wasn't alone. *If we can figure out the link. We move closer to Oz behind the curtain.*

Jaydon drifts through the kitchen. He treads towards the refrigerator and its word magnets, abuzz with an electric hum. Jaydon's heartbeat quickens, yet he remains calm.

He rearranges the metallic letters: 'HI MR DAN DOLL FASE.' Now spells: 'HAROLD MANSFIELD.' *Down the yellow brick road we go.*

Jaydon takes several photos. The words cast a reflection in the camera's lens. Click—a haze of white flash.

*　*　*

The First Garrison is a criminal court that lies in the central area—formally known as The Central Criminal Court of Justice, since the nineteenth century.

The Garrison has hosted some of the most infamous trials in this nation's history. May that be the conviction of serial murderers, the shenanigans of eccentric authors, or the prosecution of East side gangsters.

The first building traces its origins back to the seventeenth century, constructed as a sessions house to handle the growing number of criminal trials. Following the next two centuries, they added several courtrooms to accommodate the increasing number of cases.

In the late nineteenth century, architects drew up proposals for a new building, owing to the dilapidation of Greengate Prison next door.

Both buildings underwent demolition and reconstruction to form a lavishly fitted Neo-Baroque style creation. The Lady of Justice perched atop, blindfolded, with a sword in one hand and the scales of justice in the other.

Caitlyn moves towards the front entrance of this building. She has made bail just like Lyle said she would.

He and the rest of Caitlyn's legal team try to protect her from the barrage of flashbulbs and microphones. The media is in pursuit.

It seems like a hundred voices speaking at once. 'Mrs Colburn, how does it feel to be released on bail?'

'Have you spoken to your children since your husband's death?'

'Who is taking care of them?'

Caitlyn tries to block everything out. The buzzing ambience is an atmospheric half-muted chorus as the sounds of the cameras make a distant clack. The flashes become dreamlike, soft off-white circles, fading, fading, fading into complete whiteness...

* * *

Déjà vu, as Caitlyn makes that infamous stroll towards Benjamin. He sits at the kitchen table, immersed in files.

On hearing her enter, he looks up, only to see himself standing there. It is Caitlyn, who now sits in his place, offering a perplexing stare towards a very bleak and bloody Benjamin holding the gun.

She then laughs. She continues laughing uncontrollably, hysterically.

Benjamin glumly points. He fires!

* * *

Caitlyn wakes from her nightmare with a sharp gasp. The bleak vacuum of night engulfs her. Perspiration covers her clothing with a thin film. She rises from her bed and moves to the window of the five-star hotel, overlooking the breathtaking view of the inner city.

Caitlyn scrunches her toes into the hotel room's top-grade wool carpet. She thinks of all the other hotels around the world where she has done this very thing. Tokyo, Río de Janeiro, Amsterdam, Cape Town, Prague, Berlin, New York, Ubud. Each place possesses a unique feel, texture, fragrance, and palette.

Once night falls, the white glow or soft warmness of street lamps deliver backlight to the statues, monuments, and landmarks. A variation of hues and tones accompany either vibrant digital screens or signage. Motorbikes and cars move amongst luminousness, headlights ablaze amidst the sounds and smells—each place has its own rhythm, bringing forth a story for the night.

Yet, she always gravitated back here—the peaks of the modern municipality peppered with the valleys of The Slums.

She reminisces about the young, idealistic lawyer she married—a charismatic natural leader of conviction who inspired others through his human rights causes.

Somewhere along the lines, things changed. The lines became blurred. Then he moved beyond them...

❀ ❀ ❀

Benjamin resigned from his human rights causes for a career at Burling and Reed, where he worked for the defence. A firm with a reputation of playing dirty and not necessarily choosy regarding who they represented. She heard stories through the legal grapevine of their clients being freed through bribery and witness intimidation.

One particular night, she woke to hear raised voices in her living room. Caitlyn moved downstairs and found her husband in a heated discussion with a very dubious-looking man. It later turned out this man was an oligarch with known connections to the Russian mafia.

Soon after, there was a gun in the house. 'For protection,' he said—the irony.

What happened to that idealistic young lawyer? Over time, Caitlyn watched as that person slipped further and further away from her. Consumed by greed, yet rewarded for it.

❀ ❀ ❀

This did not remove the love she had for her husband. Deep down, he was still a good man. He was a wonderful father who loved his family. She would never think of doing anything like this. *So, what happened?* Her husband is gone.

55

She thinks of her poor children. The pain that they must be feeling right now. Inconsolable grief overwhelms her. The tears flow.

THE ARTIST

An artist's brush dabs and slashes at a blank canvas, creating broad strokes on its surface. A dragonfly buzzes around rays of sunlight that seep through the window, illuminating microscopic specs of dust. There is a radio podcast playing in the distance, some sort of discussion programme.

'I've lived in Hatham all my life. I can't believe how bad things have become. People are losing hope.

'Yes, there have always been tensions between this community and the police, but I don't blame the cops. We're responsible for our own lives.

'The police are only as effective as the rules they obey and what the government that enforces those rules allows.'

Another voice says, 'We solve these problems with strong community infrastructure, beginning with prioritising the home. The family unit is key. Then we can tackle the drugs plaguing the neighbourhood.'

'I agree. Removing the drugs from our streets is also paramount. These criminals have become role models. They seem to evade justice, literally getting away with murder,' says the first voice.

A third voice chimes in. 'Yasiel, we all respect you. The work you do with the kids in Kendersford makes you a hero. Yes, the community infrastructure is key.

'But let's not pretend we don't know the individuals responsible for poisoning this region and corrupting the youths. People are just too scared to act. It's time to take back the community...'

A knock on the front door causes the artist to stop mid-flow. The woman holding the brush is Ilana Lynch. This is the enigmatic figure who stood near the window the other night whilst it rained. She is also Jaydon's wife.

Ilana casually wears a tatty off-white tee shirt and a paint-splattered denim dungaree. She rises reluctantly from her canvas to answer the door.

A closer examination of the studio reveals tanned designer faux brick walls dressed with a scattering of accomplished art. There are also beautiful scrap metal sculptures and canvas portraits.

Love, passion, and occasionally pain and rage guide the creation of greatness on display. Completed by a woman used to figuring out life's answers through her creations.

Ilana opens the door as far as the attached chain will allow. She stares at Jaydon through the gap with intense silence. Ilana closes the door and catches her breath.

Jaydon waits attentively as his better half unfastens the chain. She opens the door with an array of emotions—first anger, then a glimpse of love. Hope turns to despair, then weariness. Ilana slams the door back in his face.

A wounded Jaydon stays rooted for a few moments. He turns and begins to trod away slowly. Then a creek. Jaydon turns to find a half-opened door with a stream of light seeping through.

❋ ❋ ❋

'Coffee?' Ilana asks.

'Please.'

Ilana runs tap water into the electric kettle. Jaydon admires one of her paintings hung on the kitchen wall, an abstract, formless piece. This painting has attracted several prospective buyers over the years. She never sold it.

'This is wonderful,'

I don't think he has ever said that about this painting; she thinks.

'Your work is incredible. I should have told you more often.'

Ilana prepares Jaydon's coffee with her back turned to him—the tension oozing from her. 'I used to tell Sophia that she'd grow up to be more talented than me. I used to tell her she could be anything she wanted.'

Jaydon freezes upon hearing her name spoken aloud.

He then finds his voice. 'So, listening to the radio or music still helps you work?'

'Yes.'

Jaydon observes her paint-splattered overall. 'Have you created anything interesting lately?'

She stops preparing coffee and raises her head to gaze into the distance. 'I'm not sure, maybe.'

She turns for a moment. Even without makeup, there is no denying how striking this woman is. The long dark hair, tanned olive skin, and brown piercing eyes reveal a mixture of beauty and intensity. There is also an arty punk-rock edge that hasn't been completely softened by time. The beginning of dark circles appears under her eyes. They speak simultaneously

'I should have–'

'Jaydon, you know that–'

The kettle has boiled. The simmering sound now subsides, breaking the intensity for a moment.

'Detectives Hobbes and Rousseau continue to share information,' Ilana says.

'Well, of course.' Jaydon glances outside the window where some young teenagers returning from school cavort harmlessly. Ilana pours steaming water into a glass, coffee granules at its core.

'Are you keeping an eye out for anything irregular in the area?'

'Every time you call, you ask me this.'

'And you're still testing the alarm every week, right?'

'I'm taking care of it!' She slams her palms into the nearby kitchen surface. Ilana now takes up the cup and throws it across the room. It smashes against the white wall, leaving a stain of black liquid. The silence is deafening. She turns her back to him once more. Ilana has yet to cry.

Jaydon looks at her with deep, sad eyes. His hands are raised, and fingers are outstretched. He then pulls away.

*. *. *.

Jaydon has travelled upstairs. Ilana trails a few steps behind. He stops by a room. The door handle sign reads, 'AN ANGEL AWAITS, YOU MAY ENTER', with a caricature angel above the words.

Jaydon clenches the door handle as he exhales. After a while, he loosens his grip, then gently turns the sign over to read, 'HORMONAL TEENAGER KEEP OUT', with a skull and two crossbones above it.

*. *. *.

He looks at Ilana knowingly and moves along the downstairs corridor towards the front entrance. Jaydon opens the door and turns to her. There are no words to be said. He moves away and out of sight. She closes the door behind him and re-applies the chain.

Ilana turns and braces herself against the door. Finding it hard to hold herself up, she collapses into a heap on the wooden floor.

• 12 •

THE VOICE

Jeremiah Cain, a commanding presence, sits on a park bench sporting a trimmed bohemian goatee and neatly quaffed grey hair. He watches the scene before him through piercing eyes, which you cannot determine if they are blue or grey.

This summer was hot and bright, preceded by an autumn that, though the days are becoming shorter, the sun remains in attendance. The trees' last attempts to derive energy from its foliage, producing a vivid array of red, burgundy, and orange leaves.

A young couple cavort harmlessly. A woman moves off briskly from an adjacent park bench, returning to work from her lunch break. There are others going through the motions of the everyday routine.

The screen of the digital device in Cain's hands displays lists of names and addresses, all with telephone numbers, addresses, dates of birth, psych profiles, the works.

Wearing gloves, Cain retrieves a disposable mobile phone from its box. He dials. The distant sound of the phone rings at the other end.

*. *. *.

Exhausted doctors, frantic paramedics, and a mixture of sick and injured patients all add to the hustle and bustle of Central City Hospital's ER.

The voice over the tannoy system blends with the already abundant background ambience. This includes beeping electronic machines, clanking hospital beds, and distant ambulance sirens.

Dr Isaiah Carpenter is wearing blue scrubs and a trendy crucifix around his neck. He glances down at his mobile phone—a withheld number accompanying the phone's ringing. Isaiah raises the device to his ear and answers with the press of a button. 'Hello.'

*. *. *.

It is as if Cain is addressing Isaiah in person. His eyes focused, and his steely gaze steady. 'Isaiah Carpenter?'

'Yes.'

'Isaiah Lucas Carpenter?'

'Is this...? –'

'A = 1 or 0, Em = 1 or 4, kill or die, make your choice,' Cain says. He listens intently to static at the end of the line. Moments pass. Satisfied, he ends the call.

Cain removes the phones chip and crushes it in his grip. He then steps on the burner after dropping it to the floor. Cain lowers and scoops up the discards and throws all the pieces in a nearby bin before calmly walking away.

*** * ***

Jaydon sits playing finger drums at his office desk, thinking about the strange series of events. *Something tells me this is just the beginning.*

He rotates in his swivel chair, gazing through the office's glass ceiling to the heavens of The King's Court. 'A little help here? No, I didn't think so.'

He retrieves all the reports and begins a meticulous examination. *There's got to be something we missed.*

The boxes that surround Jaydon are plentiful. He finesses a file and sees a memo with the headline: 'To: R.J Richardson, vice CEO.'

'From: Harold Mansfield, Senior Scientist.'

'Department of Research and Development,'

'Subject: Do the Morals and Ethics of Our Company Stand True?'

Jaydon inspects the first paragraph and then the subsequent two. There are errors that a man of Harold's intelligence would not produce. The discrepancies might be intentional. What were Gavin's words? *This man may have an impressive array of letters after his name, but grammar is not his strong suit.*

Jaydon hastily notes down each incorrect letter in the entire document. These letters form an array of discombobulated letters.

The detective channels his focus. Upon viewing the letters in reverse, they form two words. These two words provide a name, 'Isaiah Carpenter'. He leaps out of his seat and charges down the corridor towards Gavin's office.

• 13 •

BAPTISM OF FIRE

The red circle of the traffic light provides no deterrent to Gavin and Berg, who race towards one of the four known Isaiah Carpenter addresses. The wailing police siren and flashing lights of the unmarked vehicle make a statement. Get the hell out of my way!

Berg has been a DCI for three years. Unlike Jaydon, he became a plain-clothed officer through The National Detective Programme. He knew the work your way-up the ranks route wasn't for him.

For this reason, he has felt an onus to prove his chops and has assisted with several important arrests as a detective inspector before becoming a DCI.

* * *

Something inside of Gavin has never fully taken to Berg. Maybe it is him trying too hard. *Or maybe it is something else.* Though he can't dispute the man's work ethic and formidable record. He glances to his left whilst approaching a crossroads. 'Clear!'

Four people with the same full name. *What are the odds?* Pretty good, considering this is an urban agglomeration of thirteen million. The Isaiah, who is already in custody, is being watched—a twenty-seven-year-old AI programmer.

The unmarked vehicle that Gavin and Berg are driving screeches to a standstill. They spring from the car and an armed response vehicle comes to an abrupt halt directly in front of them.

Authorised firearm officers, Finn Owens and John Avery, exit the vehicle, rifles in hand. Gavin approaches. 'What the hell is this?!'

Avery, the older officer, speaks up. 'Sir, we received authorisation from–'

'I don't care who gave the order. Jesus, what do you think this is, some kind of raid? You guys stay here.'

The younger officer, Owens, complies with little resistance. Avery seems more reluctant.

Gavin and Berg hasten up the driveway to the two-bedroom home. 'Despite what I just said. Prepare for anything,' Gavin says. He bangs the door.

A woman in her thirties opens up with a look of concern. Gavin flashes his badge. 'I'm DSI Gavin Reece from Major Crimes. Does Isaiah Carpenter live here?'

'Yes, I'm Eloise, his partner. What's this about?'

'Is he home?'

Eloise subconsciously raises her hand to her heart. She turns to call her other half. 'Babe.'

Berg's hand hovers over the gun in his holster. There is a tense silence.

Isaiah makes his way to the front door. Though young and fit-looking, he walks and hops with the aid of a crutch owing to a broken leg—a mountain climbing accident. Isaiah scans the scene before him in a state of confusion. 'Can I help you?'

Gavin finds it hard to hide his disappointment. *This is not our guy.*

* * *

Jaydon enters the hospital's main area. He speaks to Gavin through his hands-free earpiece.

'We've rounded up two Isaiahs, but I doubt either is our guy. On route to the third. What's your location?'

'I'm already at the hospital.'

'Be careful.'

Jaydon ends the call abruptly. He stops and assesses the scene, searching the crowds for anything suspicious.

He now moves towards a young doctor doing her rounds. Glancing at her name tag, which reads, 'Dr Rebecca Howard'. He flashes his badge. 'I need to speak to Isaiah Carpenter.'

There is a micro expression that emerges across Doctor Howard's face. A look of concern. 'He's just finishing his shift.'

Jaydon scans the crowd of frantic doctors and nurses, swamped with sick people and reluctant visitors. He spots a man wearing blue hospital scrubs and carrying a large bag over his shoulder.

Jaydon drifts away from Dr Howard and in Isaiah's direction. Their eyes lock from across the room—a flicker of glimpses amidst the crowd's movement. Through nothing but pure instinct, Jaydon knows.

Isaiah manhandles a nearby cleaner, doing his rounds. On a tier of the cleaner's trolley, there is industrial cleaning fluid. He briskly retrieves a hypodermic needle from his bag and injects it into the bottle, drawing a reddish-pink liquid. Isaiah holds the needle to the cleaner's neck with one hand whilst restraining him with the other.

Jaydon un-holsters his gun and directs it at Isaiah, who hides behind the cleaner. 'Police!' Panic from the crowd ensues.

Dr Howard's expression is that of shock as she bears witness to the scene being laid out in front of her. Isaiah slowly retreats, bringing his reluctant hostage with him. He locks eyes with Jaydon in a stand-off.

The Doctor throws the cleaner aside. He then bulldozes through a nearby rear exit.

Jaydon remains in close pursuit. He weaves through the crowd of panicking people. 'Out of the way!'

Jaydon bursts through the door. In this section of the building, there is a circular staircase with no back entrances.

He looks upwards to find Isiah on the third floor. A glance at a nearby map informs him he's moving towards the fire escape. Jaydon pursues, taking the steps three at a time.

The beams of sunlight momentarily blind Jaydon as he barges through the fire entrance of the hospital's third floor. He spots Isaiah below, through the grids of the rusted brown Victorian gothic fire escape under his feet—the bolts and hinges of this late nineteenth-century architecture bang and clatter as Jaydon lays chase.

Jaydon touches the ground and remains in pursuit of Isaiah ahead. He bobs and weaves through silhouettes and the busy road of abruptly halted traffic that beep their horns in angry disapproval.

A slightly tired Jaydon slows to a stop at the corner. He carefully manoeuvres at angles, making small steps. Jaydon attacks vulnerable points by raising his gun. He scans the area—a back alley, littered and desolate.

His eagle eyes discover a broken lock on the door of a nearby church. Jaydon moves towards it.

The detective stops at the side of the church's entrance. He turns his hips towards the wall and covers the corners once again before moving into the church.

Isaiah is up ahead. There he waits, like a twisted version of a bride at the altar.

The luminescent stained-glass windows of the building encase angels, saints, and other pious characters who watch the scene play out before them.

During the Middle Ages, the poor were mostly illiterate and could not afford Bibles. The depiction of biblical events in stained glass windows provided a way for them to take lessons from the book's teachings.

Jaydon slowly stalks the figure at the far end of the church, measuring his movements. The echoes of his footsteps add an extra layer of tension to the overbearing silence. Silence where you could hear a pin drop.

As Jaydon moves closer, he notices that the large bag lies open on Isaiah's far left. However, one of its contents remains in his grasp.

Isaiah is holding a can of gasoline! A cartoon flame with a red diamond plastered across it. He raises his hands above his head and pours like a thirsty athlete throwing a bottle of water over himself after a game.

He flings the can aside and removes a lighter from his pocket. Jaydon slows to a stop and lowers his aim. Blood drips from somewhere on Isaiah to the altar floor, where he stands perfectly still.

Jaydon breaks the silence. His voice echoes off the beautifully preserved archaic walls. 'Isaiah, I need you to put the lighter aside right now.'

Isaiah stares right through Jaydon. He is like a coil ready to spring.

'Come on now. Just a simple movement, like this, see.' Maintaining eye contact. Jaydon kneels slightly and places his weapon gently on the floor.

'Hey man, whatever is happening in your life. Whatever you feel you can't fix. This is not the answer.'

Isaiah offers a twisted smirk as Jaydon moves towards him. He turns his arms outwards to reveal this now infamous mathematical formula carved artistically along each inner forearm. The markings make blood drops on the ground. This stops Jaydon in his tracks.

Dr Isaiah Carpenter says, 'I indeed baptise you with water unto repentance: but he that cometh after me is mightier than I, whose shoes I am not worthy to bear: he shall baptise you with the Holy Ghost and with fire!'

The flick of the lighter switch is deafening. He is instantly alight! A ball of fire! Isaiah spreads his arms wide, like The Lord Saviour. The saints and angels encased within the glass continue watching. Burning flames reflected through their gaze.

• 14 •

SCIENCE OR FAITH

Dr Howard is standing with Jaydon and Gavin in the corri-dor. The quarter moon of dark under her eyes is physical proof of yet another unappreciated sixteen-hour day. She holds Isaiah's clipboard tightly in her grasp.

She had been Isaiah's colleague for close to three years. They shared a bond. Though not romantically inclined, she wanted it to be that way. Despite his religious beliefs.

Recently, she sensed he was going through something. He mentioned he was receiving counselling, but this. *Oh Isaiah, what have you done?* She turns to the detectives. 'He suffered burns on over seventy percent of the body. There was a large amount of infection. This, combined with the complications. We made the last moments as comfortable as possible for him.'

Rebecca hears her own voice, but it is as if it is coming from someone else. She now knows how it feels to receive terrible news concerning a loved one who didn't make it. She pauses for a moment, composing herself.

'I take it he was a close colleague?' Gavin asks.

'He was a friend. The friend I knew would never have done something like this, not in a million years. Now, if you would excuse me, I need to notify his next of kin.' Rebecca Howard is ready to move off.

Jaydon arrests her stride, a light stroke to the arm that guides her. 'I'm sorry for your loss.' She nods, then walks away, trying to remain resolute.

* * *

Jaydon paces back and forth along the hospital corridor. He then experiences a sudden flash of recollection...

* * *

Isaiah was in flames. Jaydon rushed forward and dragged a huge cloth from a nearby table. He covered the burning man and doused out the blaze.

* * *

'This morning, I was with Ilana. I could have saved him if I had arrived here one hour sooner. Maybe Dominic was right. Maybe I'm not ready.'

'Well, it's not Dominic's call. It's mine.'

Jaydon moves away. Gavin glances at his watch. 'You're going to his home?'

Jaydon turns. He nods.

'Berg, several officers, and forensics went over it with a fine-tooth comb. They found nothing. No anagrams, equations, or fingerprints of worth. You've gone through everything here twice.'

'Oh, there is something. We're just not seeing it.'

* * *

Jaydon has been in Isaiah's home for a while. Nearby, his jacket is lying on the floor. He has undone his tie. He stands in the middle of the room and evaluates his surroundings.

On a nearby shelf is an unusual piece of African art. He moves towards it and surveys closely. It is a large, dark brown wooden creature with a deformed head that is looking and pointing directly at a bookshelf in the far corner.

Isaiah's reading collection contains a diverse array of literature. The likes of Dostoyevsky, Dumas, and Herbert share company with medical books a few shelves below. All are neatly filed in alphabetical order, dewy system, or colour-coded, depending on the category.

A portion of Isaiah's reading materials is philosophical and religious text. This includes The Upanishads, The Koran and, of course, The Bible. This catches Jaydon's attention.

He retrieves The Holy Book and opens it attentively. The inner cover reads, 'Dedicated to Isaiah, a man of science who has never lost faith. From Father David'.

• 15 •

THE PRIEST AND THE KUNG FU MASTER

Elsbury Cathedral is a sight to behold. The consolidation of buttresses, domes, stained glass windows, and spirals meld to create a sense of sublimity. This is the type of building that makes you question how humans ever managed such a majestic feat.

Jaydon and Father David stroll the exterior path alongside the Romanesque-Gothic building, framed by plants and autumn foliage. The decorative arcades and similar neighbouring architectural structures add to the scenery.

'Father, Isaiah had no living relatives. You're listed as next of kin. I thought you might be able to shed some light on why he would do something like this?'

'Isaiah confided in me, yes...' The priest contemplates for a moment. 'Well, our discussions took place outside of confession, so—'

Jaydon notes reluctance. He steers the father's arm to a stop mid-speech.

'Please, I need your help.'

Father David glances downward towards his black leather-bound Bible, which he lightly grasps close to him. He offers a self-satisfied nod. They resume movement.

'Isaiah was a devout Catholic who recently faced an ethical dilemma. A crisis of faith, if you will. We discussed his work. The people he couldn't save. It was hard for him.'

Another priest walks by and offers a wave to the father. He responds in kind.

'There was one patient, a boy named Ricky, who had an advanced progressive illness and was in excruciating pain. More pain than you or I could imagine. Have you ever witnessed someone decline in this way?'

Jaydon recollects his mother's passing for a reason unbeknownst to him...

* * *

The year Sophia was born was the year Frederica, Jaydon's mother, left this earth. She did not suffer and passed peacefully in her sleep. She was just fifty-one years old.

Even Jaydon's father made an appearance. He offered his condolences. 'I'm sorry, Jaydon. I'm sorry for everything.'

The exchange was extremely emotional for them both. The conversation concluded with Jaydon promising himself that he would never be the man his father was.

*. *. *.

'No, I have not.'

'Though you're aware that sometimes a person can suffer for months before their soul finds release. I prayed for him.

'During his rounds, Isaiah checked up on Ricky. They formed a bond.' The priest admires the autumn-coloured leaves of a nearby Field Maple tree that litter the ground.

'One night, Ricky's mother called Isaiah. She couldn't bear to watch her son suffer anymore and just needed it to end. There was no one else; by now, she often confided in Isaiah.

'He came to me asking for advice about what he should do. I advised him of our obligation to relieve suffering when we could. We should never confront the problem by taking the life of the afflicted. It is not our place.' The two men come to a halt outside the cathedral entrance.

'By morning, Ricky was gone. He passed away peacefully during the night. An accidental dose of morphine was administered.'

'Did he say anything?'

'He didn't have to, I knew. The whole thing got swept under the carpet after a brief investigation that went nowhere. This seemed to make Isaiah even more unhappy. It felt as if he wanted to be punished.'

'He was conflicted. Father, was Isaiah a part of any fanatical groups, a cult maybe?'

'There's only one that I know of.' Father David holds his bible aloft. They both manage a brief chuckle.

'I believe he was undergoing some sort of therapy, but I was reluctant to pry.'

'I see.'

The Priest calmly examines Jaydon. 'You remind me of him.'

'Me, how so?'

'Do you have spiritual beliefs? Faith?'

Jaydon senses something in the priest that he has only ever seen in one other person: a deep self-realisation and connection with the universe.

He looks to be in his mid-fifties. Roughly around the same age as his grandfather Joseph, when he and grandmother Gertrude took him in.

* * *

Their feet glided across the wooden floor like dancers whilst their upper bodies blocked, punched, chopped, and parried vicious blows. Jaydon and G-Pa Joseph were sparring in The Dojo.

Painted on the wooden floor within the centre of the rectangular space was a circle divided by dual teardrops, one white and the other black. Each teardrop contained a circle with the opposites colour—the yin and yang symbol.

Hung on the walls were Bō staffs, Sai weapons, and swords. The entrance into the space was Amado sliding wooden doors. It was as if we had stepped back in time to a traditional mix of a Japanese and Chinese abode. The urban exterior and city ambience of the modern West further augmented the fusion.

The fighting style, Kung Fu, was not the pretty moves you would associate with the movies or a Wu Shu demonstration. Southern Mantis is an aggressive, powerful form of close-quarter combat.

They handled the highly technical swift movements with power and speed. The hammer fist, phoenix eye, elbows, chops, gao choi punch, wing block, and tiger claw were all technically displayed. Their bodies hardened through years of clashing bones and hitting pieces of wood in a repetitive motion to condition.

The nineteen-year-old Jaydon was no match for Joseph, who was forty years his senior. Jaydon went high, but Joseph countered and took him down with an armlock and sweep kick. There he lay, winded and defeated.

'How did I beat you?'

'You're too quick.'

G-Pa contemplated his answer. 'Hmmm.' He walked away, hands clasped behind his back.

Joseph was a carpenter by trade and highly well-read. This was a man who could converse with the most ardent intellectual.

When Jaydon's grandparents took him in, he found it hard to settle. He was unruly, playing up at school. He often became embroiled in fights.

One night, he overheard G-Pa and his daughter conversing over the phone. 'A child needs his mother.' Then silence whilst he listened patiently. 'Yes, I understand. If you want me to discipline the boy, I have to do it my way.'

The next day, G-Pa's mini-truck was waiting for him outside the school. Jaydon approached with some trepidation. 'What are you doing here?'

'Get in.'

G-Pa's teacher, Sifu Huang, left him the dojo before returning to Hong Kong. Sifu Joseph taught many people in the community, which earned him the status of a local hero.

Jaydon was still unsure why G-Pa closed the doors to the school. One theory was a student fatally killed someone in an altercation, and he felt responsible.

G-Pa rolled up the metal shutters of The Dojo and opened the door. He then turned to Jaydon. 'You arrive here directly after school. We train once you finish your homework. This will be your second home for the next five years.'

Jaydon hated the training at first. G-Pa's persistence for perfection resulted in Jaydon being severely disciplined. There were also obsessive rules that he had to obey.

Yet, after a while, he found that he truly valued the structure. He began excelling at school. It turned out that overcoming the adversity of triangle-type press-ups, horse stances, reciting forms, and conditioning, provided resilience, mental strength, and confidence.

Jaydon eventually realised that these lessons were not only an education in martial arts but also life. The bond between him and G-Pa became unbreakable.

During the wake of his mother, he wished to escape the many condolences offered by well-meaning people. A tired, suited, and tied, twenty-seven-year-old Jaydon travelled upstairs to Frederica's room. He gravitated towards the window.

Jaydon stood in the exact place that his mother had, all those years ago, where she overlooked the chaos of the riots on the streets below.

I used to believe you were selfish, sending me away. Now I realise you were the most selfless person I have ever known. *Where are you now?*

A knock on the door took him out of his thoughts. G-Pa moved towards him. 'Ilana is looking for you downstairs.'

Jaydon turned with tears in his eyes. 'What're your thoughts on the universe, G-Pa? Of God?'

Jaydon's grandfather glided his fingers along a nearby bedside table. 'I made this from a dying ash tree. The table's substance is wood. The properties of wood are cellulose fibres. Those fibres derive from microscopic cells. The formation of cells involves molecules. Atoms come before this, subatomic particles before them, but to begin, there are quarks. What comes before quarks?' G-Pa offered a smile whilst a single tear ran down his cheek.

'Scientist will continue searching for that elusive substance beyond their grasp. You could call it God or an ultimate truth embedded with love. The name is inconsequential. What matters is that it is there.'

✻ ✻ ✻

Jaydon looks the priest in the eyes. 'I'm afraid that faith is a luxury I can no longer find.'

'Maybe you need help with your search.'

Jaydon measures up this man standing before him. This man, clothed in black. His eyes invite him in.

'The most valuable thing in the world was taken from me, ripped from my life. Where was God then?'

Father David contemplates for a short while.

'Sometimes, no words can be said to ease a person's suffering. No act of kindness will remove their pain. Should the need arise for solace, somewhere to shelter from the darkness to draw strength from the light, these doors remain open.' He raises a hand towards the cathedral's entrance. The chiming of the distant bells is the only sound to be heard.

'Thank you for your time, Father.'

Father David watches Jaydon attentively as he departs. 'What was their name?'

Jaydon halts but does not turn.

'The one who was taken?'

His face mirrors pain. 'The dead no longer have names.' Jaydon strides away as the bells continue to clang and chime from the steeple on high.

· 16 ·

DOLL FACE

Jaydon sits at his desk. He tries to distillate these peculiar events. Whoever put this in motion is methodical, with a firm idea of how things will transpire.

So, what is the fundamental question to ask? *How are they doing this? What are they trying to say? Or is it simply why?*

He is finding it hard to continue focusing. There is something about this morning's conversation that has permeated his consciousness.

He meditates on his own state of being. The job has provided a distraction, but most certainly not a remedy. *Maybe it's time to face the inevitable.*

He opens his phone wallet, and within lays the blue origami unicorn he possessed earlier. That's when he sees her, the Adolescent Girl. There, right in front of him. *She's not real.* His mind regresses to a string of memories in time...

Jaydon stood tense as he listened to the voice on the other end of the phone receiver. A voice that was ominous, monotone, and devoid of emotion. Clear cut, close to the King's English, but not quite.

'Don't bother with a trace. The line's decoded.'

'Who is this?' Jaydon asked.

'You know who I am.'

※ ※ ※

The first was on Halloween. An abduction of a seventeen-year-old by the name of Abigail Rose. She was last seen returning home from college. A few days later, the police found her body five miles away from where she lived.

Perched by a nearby oak tree was a doll, similar in style to the Japanese ball-jointed dolls made for teenagers. It was looking directly over at the crime scene and bore a striking resemblance to the victim.

CSI's found no trace evidence on the victim or at the scene. However, they discovered something quite startling. The doll's hair belonged to Abigail.

A further abduction and murder took place three months later—a sixteen-year-old by the name of Lucy Walker. The layout of the scene was almost identical to Abigail's, including a nearby doll that resembled the victim with her actual hair woven into the scalp.

Within a year, there were two more victims, both teenagers. The King's Court was called in on the second kill.

Jaydon felt a personal connection. The girls being abducted were not much older than Sophia.

They couldn't catch a break. The Doll Face Killer was too methodical and organised. Jaydon finally got something.

One of the initial avenues of inquiry was to track down orders for any materials used to make the dolls and machinery. They found nothing. So, Jaydon ordered the cyber team to closely monitor the dark web for anything unusual.

There was an individual who purchased a certain polyurethane resin from a European company in real-time. This alone was not enough to raise any suspicions. However, it turned out that this business also created 3D doll-making machines to spec.

Frustrated that this person hid behind anonymity, Jaydon had the cyber team hack into their computer, unbeknown to Gavin, Berg, or anybody else. He wanted to be sure before notifying them.

It seems his instincts were correct, as this individual also purchased one of the specialised doll printing machines several months before the killings began. The IP address led to a physical location and name, which was Ian Moone.

The King's Court tore the place down. They found equipment and cash, but nothing else: no fingerprints, no identification, no trace samples. Not even the landlord knew his identity. Ian Moone was no one. Ian Moone was in the wind.

One day, Sophia completed her piano lesson with Mrs Haines. Ilana was busy organising her fifth exhibition. She phoned Sophia to tell her she would be late to pick her up.

Sophia said it was okay as she could walk, and it was a nice day. 'It's not far.'

Sophia never returned home. Two weeks later, Jaydon received a package containing his daughter's doppelgänger doll. The hair of the doll was a DNA match. Where was the body? Where was Sophia?

Jaydon turned over the entire megalopolis, searching. He broke police rules like they didn't matter, and they didn't. This was his daughter. But Moone was gone, because Ian Moone is I am no one.

* * *

Jaydon's grip on the phone tightened. The page on his digital newspaper device displayed the headline, 'Policeman's Daughter Abducted by Doll Face Killer'.

* * *

Doll Face sat in a dimly lit room—an Ominous Figure cloaked in the shadows.

'Maybe you need proof. She has a birthmark on her right shoulder. That necklace, the one your wife made with her initials. It's very nice, one of a kind, right?'

There was a sharp intake of breath on the other end of the line.

'I make things too, toys, dolls mostly.' Several disturbing-looking dolls, momentarily bald, lay on a shelf—the type of things made for horror movies.

* * *

'What have you done?'

'You already know the answer to that, don't you? I can't think of anything worse than the agony of not knowing.'

Ilana drifted to a standstill in the doorway. You just had to take one look at her to know she hadn't slept for days.

'Take a step back and consider what you're doing right now. If anything's happened–'

'You know the answer, detective. You have to. The only reason you got anywhere near me is because you think like I do. We're the same.'

If Jaydon could climb into the phone line and materialise at the other end to beat this man to death, he would. 'I'm nothing like you.' Jaydon then revised his tone, knowing that Doll Face had the upper hand. 'Listen to me–'

'The one difference being I'm free whilst you remain captive, handcuffed by the restraints of laws and societal norms. Prisoner by choice. Don't worry; when the time comes, I'm going to set you free.'

Ilana rushed forward and grabbed the phone. 'Hello. Hello... Where is she? Where is she?! If you harm one more hair on her head. You hear me! Hello?!' The line went dead.

* * *

'Hey, you okay? Lost you there for a bit,' Gavin says. His question gradually draws Jaydon out of his melancholic stupor.

Jaydon rises from his seat and moves away, out of sight. Gavin looks on with concern.

* * *

Jaydon returns to his apartment. He neglects to turn on the light switch. Though, the exterior street lamp and intermittent night strobes of pink and blue neon provide some illumination.

He appraises his surroundings. All this research, the police files. *A waste of time.*

Helplessness overcomes him. He hurls over the table, spilling all its contents onto the floor! He hurtles a chair across the unlit room with extreme force! It crashes against the wall. Jaydon's fist goes straight through the living room door!

He then slumps into a nearby chair, now spent. He broods in half silhouette, where the exterior light falls partially across his face.

*. *. *.

The flicker of glimmering lights enhances the stunning interior of St Albans Cathedral, showcasing Romanesque architectural lines and angles.

Father David lights a lone candle at the altar. An abundance of candles surround the singular flame. They are of various shapes, sizes, and colours. He motions a gesture of the cross before a noise suddenly draws his attention.

Father David's eyes travel into the darkness beyond. 'Who's there?' Feet shuffle in shadow. Father David moves towards the sound. 'Show yourself!'

Jaydon appears from the darkness. He stops at a distance and then finds his composure. 'Her name was Sophia.'

• 17 •

THE BURNING MAN

Jaydon and Father David each sit on a bench on opposite sides of the aisle, near the altar. They both stare straight ahead, admiring the luminous candle display before them. Light from flickering flames dance eerily across their faces.

'She was a good kid, honest, smart, wise way beyond her years, and creative, just like her mother.

'She would make origami. You know, little animals, flowers, insects. I would always keep one with me wherever I went.

'There was this case, a guy slaying teenage girls. He would leave a decrepit doll with human hair sewn into the scalp—the hair of each victim.

'I was close. So close. Too close. The moment I entered the house that night, I knew something was wrong. I could just feel it in the air. God knows where my daughter is.'

'I'm afraid he does,' the priest says. Father David has a purpose and takes honour in carrying the encumbrance of others. Though, when moments like this occur, he always wonders, *will this burden be too much to bear?*

The priest gazes into the light of the candles. This night reminds him of his missionary work abroad. When locals sat around a campfire to exchange insight, the Elders would envisage stories of travelling to other realms.

Four hundred thousand years ago, we discovered the wonders of fire. This changed things forever. Circadian rhythms shifted, and brain sizes grew. *Was this the origin of our predators now becoming our prey?*

Father David observes Jaydon. There is tension oozing from every pore. This man is at war with himself. What will happen to his prey?

Ilana is on the phone with Gavin, the mobile is on speaker. She holds Buddhist prayer beads lightly in her grasp. Earlier, she had been chanting *Tayata Om Bekanze Bekanze Maha Bekanze Radza Samudgate Soha.* Which roughly translates to the healing of true suffering.

'If Jaydon's home, he's not answering. Has he called?' Gavin asks.

'No.'

'I'm concerned he might fall off a cliff, Ilana.'

'A cliff is too close to the sky. Jaydon's deep in hell.'

Gavin sits in relative darkness, apart from the whitish-blue glow from the exterior street lamp, which seeps through gaps in the Venetian blinds, causing strips of luminance and shadow. He is the only person at home, as Evelyn is spending time with family.

Gavin rolls the bronze sobriety coin over the back of his knuckles into his palm. Then, he returns the gesture in a continuous motion. 'I can't tell you how often I lay awake at night. Turning over the thoughts in my mind. Was there anything else I could have done?'

'You don't need to do this.'

'Maybe so. Yet I feel compelled to. What you've gone through–'

'I wouldn't wish upon anyone. I'm doing everything I can to stay in the light. Though I'm not afraid of the dark.'

'Maybe not being afraid of the dark is the very thing we should be afraid of.'

*. *. *.

'As you would expect, I became obsessed with finding the murderer, breaking the rules to do so. As time went on, I lost objectivity. They suspended me. A fellow detective named Berg led the investigation the best he could, but it was no use.

'Detectives Hobbes and Rousseau remain on the case. The monster is in the wind.'

'To lose a child. Now Isaiah's gone. I suppose I have some idea how that feels. I would understand if there was no longer any room left for forgiveness?'

'Whose forgiveness are we talking about, Father, God's or mine?'

'Yours. When you catch this man, what then?'

'I think you know.'

Father David's gaze meets the hatred seething in Jaydon's eyes. He then glances downward at his bloodied and bruised hands.

'During my earlier years. I did missionary work in the Sahel region of Africa. For a while, I stayed with the Hinutu tribe.

'If someone commits murder and they catch the culprit. They have a ritual called the burning man.

'They locked the killer in an open-topped metal shed under direct sunlight, without food or water. The victim's family has a choice: to either save the killer or let them die a horrible death, suffocating in intense heat.

'The Hinutu believe if they let them die, the aggrieved have their revenge. Though the victim remains in the afterlife, blind and alone, waiting for someone to guide the way.

'However, if they save the culprit and show mercy, the victim regains sight, and the family can move on with their lives.'

'You believe that?'

Father David sighs thoughtfully, then contemplates. 'Vengeance is an act inspired by man's wishful fulfilments. If you kill this man out of some need for revenge, there's a chance your soul will be forever lost, and Sophia may never find the peace she deserves.'

✳ ✳ ✳

Gavin remains sitting in the dark, completing his yearly ritual. He meditates on the chipped ice cubes that float and swirl within a glass of bourbon on a nearby table next to an almost full bottle. He reaches out, fingers caressing the glass. *The job, that's where it begins...*

✳ ✳ ✳

Being a cop in Baltimore back then was like a parallel universe turned upside down. Gang banging, murders, domestic abuse, rapes, and all other gory crimes in between.

PTSD, what was that? You did your shift and then frequented the bar to drown out the horrors burnt into your brain.

Soon, the alcohol doesn't work anymore. Then what? Drugs, legal or illegal, it didn't matter? Maybe death by suicide or on the job. That's where he was heading. Then Evelyn came along.

Six months later. He was a teetotaller who attended AA meetings instead of bars.

＊ ＊ ＊

Gavin scoops up the bottle and the glass. Moves to the sink and pours the contents down the drain. He then raises the empty glass in salute of another year of sobriety.

＊ ＊ ＊

Sometime later, Gavin rolls out his yoga mat. He acutely remembers the time when one of his colleagues mentioned the multiple benefits of this ancient practice. So, he gave it a shot and has never looked back since.

His lithe body, silhouetted by moonlight, flows elastically into the asana as thunder and lightning tap on the night sky. The rain falls.

TEARS IN RAIN

Ilana sits, waiting patiently for Jaydon to call. She contemplates the burden that he volunteers to carry. A consequence of his purpose. The empath, armed with a wooden sword, embroiled in a forest of grim. Yet, he continues to slay the monsters, if not always saving the princess, whilst struggling to keep his own darkness at bay.

Jaydon has tried valiantly to remove her pain and make it his own. She shut him out. The door knocks.

*. *. *.

Ilana and Jaydon sit in the living room with the light switched off. It continues to rain—an endless composition of aqua pattering against the windowpane.

The combination of the full moon and downpour creates glimmering light that falls across their faces. Ethereal droplets of luminance flickering amongst shadowy tears.

Jaydon observes the pitter-patter of raindrops, which evokes the thought of the gleaming candle display in the church. He acknowledges the duality. 'I remember the day when Sophia was born. I stood over that hospital crib. God knows how long, just watching her sleep. That's when it hit me, how fragile life can be.

'I made a promise that nothing would harm my family. I failed.'

There was a time when Ilana, looking for someone to blame, would have condemned Jaydon, but this was not his fault. The simple fact is, he spat in the faces of the monsters. Happenstance, being Sophia, was in those woods when the monsters spat back. 'You're not to blame.'

'You asked me to leave.'

'I had to. Seeing you was like looking in a mirror. Hopelessness and despair glaring back at me through a broken reflection.'

Ilana kneels in front of Jaydon. She takes his hands and looks up lovingly into his eyes. Her following words are in Spanish. '*I'm hanging on by a thread, Jaydon, and it is about to snap. So, find him. Do what you have to do and bring our baby home to us. So, she can rest, so we can rest.*'

She then stands over him. Something in her persona goes dark. '*Or so help me, God, I will.*'

* * *

Jaydon apprehensively approaches Sophia's bedroom, which he hasn't visited since shortly after the abduction. His heart rate quickens and his fingers tremble as he reaches for the door handle.

The hanging door sign reads, 'HORMONAL TEENAGER KEEP OUT', with a skull and two crossbones hovering above. He turns the sign over to display, 'AN ANGEL AWAITS PLEASE ENTER'.

Ilana watches him lovingly whilst caressing his back. Jaydon exhales fully before turning the door handle.

The room is dark. He switches on the light. There is a mural on the far side of the wall. Sophia was a talent.

The painting contains a large self-portrait of their daughter—a bric-à-brac of animal totems with various bits of surrounding urban landscape.

Ilana gazes at the mural with joy and the opening up of surrender. She recalls when she started nurturing Sophia's creative intuition...

*. *. *.

Ilana would take Sophia to museums and art galleries around the city. She would explain the sketching and painting techniques to her. They did arts and crafts often. Origami was one of their favourite past times.

Sophia's piano skills were also progressing. She began practising more complex pieces. Sometimes, Jaydon accompanied her with his guitar whilst she played.

Whilst visiting Ilana's parents in Chicago, Sophia helped Ilana and her grandmother make jewellery to send back home for the Puerto Rican Day Parade. She glanced upwards, feeling eyes on her. 'Mother, when I grow up, I want to be an artist just like you. What do you think?'

Ilana looked at her own mother knowingly, who listened with a smile whilst looping a necklace. 'Yes, if you work hard and remain humble. It is possible to achieve your dreams.'

This was close to Sophia's twelfth birthday. Ilana made her a beautiful, natural Onex stone necklace with 'S' inscribed on its surface. Sophia said, 'I will wear it always.'

※　※　※

Jaydon drifts towards the bedside table, where there is a vast array of origami, which includes a dragonfly, a swan, and a unicorn. He tenderly opens Sophia's top drawer and discovers a red scarf on top of all the other carefully folded items.

Jaydon places the scarf to the side of his face, breathing in for a while. He stumbles to the window, scarf in hand. Setting down this precious item of clothing on the ledge.

He draws the window open, glad for the evening breeze and sound of distant traffic. The rain has subsided. It is warm for this time of year—one of those evenings where a mild breeze rustles through the trees with a whisper, making them sway.

There is a glass wind chime nearby, providing fragments of Jaydon's reflection. The chime tinkles and clangs, several pieces of broken glass mirroring different parts of his face in movement.

A sudden gush catches the scarf, scooping it out of reach before Jaydon can react. It flies up and away like a kite, dancing with the breeze before fading into the night sky.

Ilana drifts towards Jaydon, who still has his arms outstretched. She holds him close. They stand near the mural. Sophia's portrait hovers over them. They are a family once more.

❋ ❋ ❋

It's late. Jaydon and Ilana are now in their own bedroom. The moon highlights Ilana's profile as she sleeps.

Jaydon kneels before her, brushes the hair from her face, and kisses her forehead. He rises and stands over her for a moment. Then moves out of sight.

• 19 •

KNOWLEDGE IS MIGHTIER THAN THE FIST

Jaydon walks through the hall of the dimly lit police library. He shares the space with one security guard lounging around upstairs, preoccupied with his iPad. A nearby clock reads *3:44 a.m.*

Whilst moving to his required destination, he revisits a specific moment in time...

❊ ❊ ❊

They drove almost two hundred miles. G-Pa Joseph had pushed Jaydon extremely hard in training earlier that morning. It was a Saturday afternoon.

The mini truck cruised to an allotted parking space near an unmissable building. Jaydon, a frustrated and tired fifteen-year-old, said, 'What is this place?'

'It's a library.'

The National Central Library—a two-hundred and eighty thousand square foot, six-floor behemoth shaped like a wedge.

This assembly, placed within Library Square, contained a landscaped and paved plaza that encompassed the entire region. A garden topped the construction on the roof, planted with trees, grass, flowering bulbs, and various perennial plants.

Inside this impressive structure was a gallery of local artists, coffee shops, a spiral staircase, and several glass elevators. The library's collection comprised six hundred thousand books and an expansive digital resource.

'Libraries are boring.'

G-Pa chuckled to himself. Then, his persona changed. He turned to Jaydon. 'Knowledge is the most powerful thing a young man can possess, even more than these.' G-Pa displayed his two calloused fists.

'You are doing well at school, Jaydon. I think there's room for improvement. Books are the great equaliser in which paths can open for you to walk through.'

Jaydon remained somewhat uninterested, though a little curious. G-Pa removed his seatbelt. 'Let's go in.'

*. *. *.

Jaydon sits at a library table with a reading light and a stack of books and research papers for company. He reads through notes on ethics, hedonism, and consequentialism.

His eyes locate a quote in which Kant said, 'In law, a man is guilty when he violates the rights of others. In ethics, he is guilty if he only thinks of doing so.' Two words from this quote catch his eye: 'law,' and 'ethics.'

He thinks of Caitlyn, *a lawyer*. Then Isaiah and Harold. *A doctor and a scientist.* Career positions in which morals, ethics, and the law play a prominent role. On occurrence, possibly at odds.

He conducts research on the four pillars of medical ethics. 'Beneficence,' 'Non-maleficence,' 'Autonomy,' 'Justice.' His mind ruminates on the word *ethics*.

Jaydon scans through a document written by a local law firm. Honing in on '1.1 What are Ethics?' He reads further.

'Ethics are principles and values, which together with rules of conduct and laws, regulate the legal profession.'

✳ ✳ ✳

Jaydon is now sitting at a table in front of a computer. He massages his eyes tiredly, then glances upwards towards the libraries clock which reads *5:08 a.m.* He recites the symbols, letters, and numbers of the equation in his mind. *Where have I seen this before?*

Jaydon types, 'maths+ethics+philosophy' into the police's powerful search engine. There are a few results—one name in particular piques his interest.

Armed with the name, Jaydon types in: 'theorems by mathematician Saravanan Vishwakarma.' There are several hundred hits. He types in the words 'Saravanan Vishwakarma's equation on morality and ethics.' It narrows down to one.

• 20 •

THE MATHEMATICIAN

For as long as I could remember, I have always seen the world mathematically. The fractions, scales, and interval ratios of music. Algebra and trigonometry, interwoven within the frames of a building.

My name is Saravanan Vishwakarma, and I was born on December 26th, 1891, in Nilgiris, Tamil, India. The exact time of my birth was unknown.

My father, Suresh, worked as a civil servant. Devika, my mother, looked after the home.

Since my dad was always working, and my older sibling, sadly, passed away before his second birthday. It was me and my mother most of the time. We were close.

She taught me about Brahmin culture and the Puranas, which are ancient texts containing stories explaining the mysteries of the universe.

My belief was that the way to decode the cosmos and reach God was through mathematics. A numerical value roots all things that have existed.

When I was eleven years old, I passed my primary examinations in English, Tamil, geography, and arithmetic with the best scores in the district.

Other subjects easily bored me, but I devoured a vast array of books by reputable mathematicians. Soon after, I discovered a way to devise sophisticated theorems and completed my school maths exams in just 47.65% of the time allocated. They regarded me as a maths prodigy.

There were some setbacks, such as my frustration, when trying to solve quintic equations in terms of radicals with $n\sqrt{}$. Then, I discovered this was an impossibility upon studying the Abel–Ruffini theorem.

My parents arranged for me to marry at twenty-three years of age. My wife, Radhika, was from Rajendram, a village close to Marudur.

A job was required to support my wife, who was now pregnant. We contacted Dipesh Chandrasekar, the founder of the Indian Mathematical Society, and asked for a position at the revenue department where he worked.

I showed him my notebooks containing mathematical analysis, number theory, infinite series, and continued fractions. He said, 'I have no intention of stifling you here. The world must learn of your genius.'

Mathematicians around India soon learned of my theories. Some doubted that it was my work, which included the district collector for Nellore and the secretary of the Indian Mathematical Society, Taarank Iyer.

I mentioned the correspondence I had with the prestigious Professor Srinivasan from Bombay. He notified them that this was indeed my findings.

They sent me to Madras to continue my research with financial aid. I wrote my first formal paper for the Journal of the Indian Mathematical Society on the properties of Bernoulli numbers.

I made communication with Oxford University mathematician Julian Beckett. He responded enthusiastically to my manuscripts, particularly my work on continued fractions.

So, I sent him a letter chock-full of theorems with the note. 'I have found a brother in maths who views my labour sympathetically.'

With the support of The Board of Mathematics, I made my way to England, where I spent close to five years. The exact time was equal to one thousand seven hundred and fifty-two days.

Beckett and I clashed in some ways. My approach to maths was much more intuitive and insightful. Beckett had a need for more rigour.

He was an ardent atheist whilst I was a Hindu Brahmin, inspired by the goddess Parvati, who came to me in my dreams. It was through Brahman's grace that I would solve mathematical problems so effortlessly, to the astonishment of my fellow mathematicians.

Chronic illness was present throughout my life. I suffered from a hepatic condition. My time on this plane was to be short.

During one of my visions from the Hindu goddess, I was told my atman would depart from my body at age thirty-three.

I delved into my life's work of interpreting the universe's secrets through mathematics—the creation of several summations derived through this frantic search.

Finally, I returned home to India to handle my affairs and ensure the financial well-being of my wife and son once I departed.

The doctor diagnosed me with tuberculosis It was determined that I had approximately one hundred and eighty-two days left to live.

Towards the end of this physical state of being, during a markedly warm night, I had a dream in which I witnessed the world as it truly was—a luminous, infinite array of harmonious numbers, symbols, fractions, and equations.

This vast radiant display of mathematics materialised into the O Mighty Lord Krishna. 'Look within, and you will find the universe,' said he.

To understand the true atman, you must first know that which hinders authenticity: the mind and emotions.

I felt inspired to create the final several of my four thousand three hundred and twenty-five theorems on this subject. This explored human emotions, motivations, and perceptions. Some of these equations were:

$$0 \leq |E_m| \leq 4$$

$$0 \leq M \leq 100$$

$$M = \frac{2.5 \cdot |Em| \cdot (ES)}{C}$$

$$Te : ES \times IS \rightarrow BL$$

$$A = \begin{cases} 1, N = \mathbf{T} \wedge F = \mathbf{T} \\ 0, N = \mathbf{F} \vee F = \mathbf{F} \end{cases}$$

The body is no more. My atman is now a minute fraction that has rejoined the numerical cosmos of ∞ = Brahman.

Jaydon stands outside the police library. The time on his mobile device reads *6:26 am*. He speed-dials Gavin and raises the device to his ear. 'I have something.'

• 21 •

NO MAN IS IMORTAL

The placement of Kings Court is directly in the central area. Jaydon stands on the rooftop of the police headquarters, which offers a three-hundred-and-sixty-degree panoramic view of the megalopolis.

Several silhouetted concrete edifices cast a shadow over neighbouring buildings of various shapes and sizes. Below, in the far distance, shimmering spheres of light blink and stretch, then drift and fade into soft focus. The orange of the sun climbs over the city, bathed in a blue hue.

There remains a level of tranquillity. Though you can feel the metamorphosis of the municipality as it emerges into life.

Jaydon absorbs the relative calm, feeling the cold air on his skin, trying to remain present. He has been thinking a lot about G-Pa Joseph recently. A wave of sadness washes over him. *No man is immortal...*

Jaydon was lying in bed. He found it hard to sleep owing to a troublesome case he was working on. There was a serial rapist operating uptown. This man was very careful not to leave any evidence behind.

To compound things, G-Pa was not well. Though he was healthier than most men his age, he developed a heart arrhythmia at birth, which had somehow caught up to him.

Jaydon could sense something was amiss before the phone rang. Ilana stirred and then rose upon hearing it. Sophia was now old enough for her own room and was fast asleep next door.

He answered the phone after the second ring. It was his grandmother, Gertrude. 'Grandma?'

'Joseph's gone, Jaydon. He's gone.'

Jaydon immediately offered to be by her side, but Gertrude insisted he leave it until the morning. She had good company around her and would be fine.

Jaydon told Ilana that he needed to clear his head. He took the Zero DSR for a spin.

The speedometer moved up to 90mph. He lost control of the bike. Jaydon was fortunate to avoid being killed and only experienced a broken arm, along with a few cuts and bruises. He earned his famous eyebrow scar as he wore his open-faced helmet when the accident occurred.

He held Ilana's hand as she sat by his hospital bed that night. Both of them were in tears.

* * *

'This never tires,' Gavin says. He moves towards Jaydon, offering a look of concern, before turning towards the view. They stand side by side, taking it all in. A reflective silence ensues.

Jaydon then turns to him. 'There was nothing more you could have done.'

Gavin feels a huge weight lift. They move away with purpose.

* * *

DSI Gavin Reece stands in front of a crime board, surveying all of what they have so far. Maps, files, notes, and photos. Linked by a criss-cross of string and coloured pins.

Jaydon is on the other side of the room. He examines the glass board and equation scrawl, pondering Saravanan Vishwakarma's final summations. *What was his goal here?*

From what he could gather, this mathematical genius was not a malicious man. His work was for the betterment of humanity. He concludes that the instigator behind this is using the equation as inspiration, not as proof of his hypothesis.

Berg sits on a nearby stool. His line of sight finds Jaydon, then Gavin. 'Am I the only one curious how he knows all this?'

'There's this invention called books. You may have heard of them,' Jaydon says.

Gavin offers a chuckle.

'A wealth of knowledge at your fingertips. Power through words on a page.'

'I don't even own a library ticket.'

'Have you even visited a library before?' Gavin asks.

'I tried once, but I came out in rashes.'

They all laugh.

Jaydon gears up to summarise his findings. The energy of the room then takes a more serious turn.

'The formula explores human behaviour. A famous Indian mathematician from the early twentieth century wrote some theorems on the subject.

'This section of his work circled around human behaviours, such as morality, motivations, and emotions.

'This equation assigns the strength of an emotion on five levels, ranging from zero to four. Zero equals nothing, and four is the most powerful. An emotion such as love, for instance.'

'Or hate,' Berg Says.

'Or hate. This is its symbol.' Jaydon points to E_m.

'Emotion provides energy for motivation.' He singles out M on the neighbouring formula.

'Measured at zero to one hundred. Motivation, at its strongest, transforms thoughts into actions and behaviours.

These behaviours are all measured by values, social norms, and our point of existence.

'This now brings us to attitude.' He points to A.

'A1 equals positive. A0 equals negative. Positive is what we would deem normal, sociably acceptable behaviour. The negative varies from antisocial to egregious or appalling.'

'The line. It's all about crossing the line,' Berg says.

'The mathematician. What was his conclusion?' Gavin asks.

'I'm not sure.'

'What's yours?' Berg asks.

Jaydon contemplates this for a moment. 'Nothing is barer than the human soul or as complex as its psyche.'

'We all have the choice to be an angel or demon,' Gavin muses.

'Or maybe there is just a killer within all of us waiting to escape,' Berg utters darkly.

22

NUMBERS ON A SPINE

DI Carter sits at a desk, taking notes from a book. Jaydon is nearby, trying to figure out the instigators' next move. None of this was random. It would have taken a huge amount of effort and planning. *So, what now?*

He observes DI Carter working away. Something that Berg mentioned earlier replays in his mind. *I don't even own a library ticket.* He ponders on this.

❦ ❦ ❦

Detective Jaydon Lynch is once again in Isaiah's home. He tries to empathise with the doctor and what he was wrestling with.

An ER professional's role is to starve off death, not instigate it. Would easing the suffering of a terminally ill patient be equivalent to the murder of a known villain absent of trial and due process? *It shouldn't be.* Isaiah crossed the line professionally. *But did he remain moral?*

Jaydon's eyes scan Isaiah's bookshelf. He recollects the countless visits to the library where he devoured vast amounts of literature, so much so that he memorised the complete Dewey system.

American librarian and educator Melvil Dewey created the Dewey system in 1873 and first published it in 1878. This is the most common library classification system in the world, adopted by universities, colleges, schools, and, of course, libraries. Librarians file fictional titles in alphabetical order under the author's surname.

Jaydon's line of sight finds one Dewey number, then another. He zooms in on book titles, words, and colour codes. Specific books have highlighted letters and the occasional number.

His thought process takes charge. Jaydon rearranges the words in his mind. The letters and numbers lift from the books' spines and float around him. They come together to form a name.

※ ※ ※

Gavin sits at his office desk. He types urgently into the glass touchpad keyboard. Jaydon tries his best to be heard over the road traffic at the other end.

'The name is Mark Summers. Followed by 7, 20, 03. I repeat 7, 20, 03. Cross-reference the numbers for an address, coordinates, date, or date of birth.'

'Running it through the system now.' Gavin conducts a search on his computer. It provides one name that matches all the information.

*. *. *.

Jaydon sits in an unmarked police car near the motorway. The drivers that zoom by are strangers to the detective. Blissfully unaware as they continue to play the lead role in their life story.

'Jaydon, I've got something. Summers, Mark. Mixed race male, 6ft 3" tall, 30 years old, eye and hair colour brown, did two tours in the Middle East War. He received his discharge over a year ago. Are you sure about this?'

'Yes, I'm positive. It was the dewy system in Isaiah's home. That's where it was hidden. What's his address?'

*. *. *.

Jaydon parks his vehicle near a mishmash of high-rise blocks, which you can describe as a perfect display of ramshackle architecture that rises from the earth of the ghetto.

Yet, there is beauty in what residents moniker The Cinderella Mansions. Concrete rickety shanty houses, all thrown on top of each other and fused into a U-shape amalgamation, with lofty ambitions to reach just a little closer to the sky.

The government built high-rise buildings for residential use following the Second World War, regarded as a swift cure for crumbled unsanitary structures and a replacement for buildings destroyed by relentless German bombings.

The buildings received an initial welcome for their improved views and affordable cost. There soon came deterioration, then crime, vandalism, and the reality of people being trapped in concrete boxes without gardens and community.

Eventually, they abandoned the brave new world experiment, whilst gentrification resulted in the transformation of several areas. Hatham is currently not one of them.

* * *

Jaydon moves quickly and quietly along the third floor of The Cinderella Mansions. He slows to a stop at Mark Summers' flat.

The detective leans against the wall just beside the door. His fists bang wood to announce his presence. 'Mark Summers, this is the police. Open up!'

He receives no reply apart from a muffled voice that sounds like a television. A barking dog in an apartment below also has something to say.

'Mr Summers, this is Detective Jaydon Lynch. Open the door right now! I need to talk to you!' Still nothing. He scans his surroundings to see if there are any bystanders.

Jaydon was not always on the rights side of the law. During his early teens, he spent significant time around criminality. The irony being, on several occasions, his unlawful education has been more helpful for his police work than when he was living in The Slums.

From his inner coat pocket, he removes a paperclip, which he straightens with his fingers. He inserts the clip into Summers' apartment door lock. He turns the pin in a clockwise circular motion until there is finally a click. Jaydon draws his weapon, pushes the door slightly ajar, and then enters.

The assumed television was, in fact, a nearby radio. The voice is that of a newsreader, providing an hourly update. None of it is good.

Jaydon is alert and moves with caution. His gun and flashlight lead the way. He knows that a highly trained soldier is potentially waiting in the shadows.

The Newsreader says, '...stabbed the victim five times in Kendersford this morning, leaving them for dead. They are in critical condition. Police are appealing for any witnesses to please come forward....'

Gavin told Jaydon to wait for backup. He ignored him, knowing the risks. A building search is dangerous. The suspect just has to wait as they lie low in several possible hiding spots.

Jaydon avoids staying too close to the wall. Brushing against plaster transmits sound. You're vulnerable to being hit by ricocheting bullets and objects piercing a thinner wall from the other side.

The Newsreader continues to provide background noise during the detective's plight. He says, '...Fully armed police patrols will be present in areas like Hatham and Pelth as part of Phase One of the War Against Crime Initiative.

'The traditional deployment of specialist firearm units has been ineffective throughout these hotspots, which has seen rises in knife and gun-related crimes to seventeen and a half percent over the last six months.

'Apparently, there has been no debate, no consultation, and no consideration to the vehement opposition that exists from community leaders and several civil rights organisations.

'If made a success, heads are keen for this to be introduced on a national level, providing firearms for every police officer nationwide in the next two years with the possibility of also arming private security provisions that work within the most affected areas.

'Phases two and three will begin shortly and will involve the stabilisation of the communities through...'

Jaydon picks out a silver dog tag lying on a wooden chair. Various weights and exercise equipment lay in a corner. A shelf props up a photo of Mark Summers and his fellow soldiers from the Middle East war.

The detective cautiously approaches the corner of the room that meets the hallway. He takes a 90-degree step away from the wall and slices into a semi-circle. He moves down the corridor towards a half-open door. Gun and flash-light leading the way.

Jaydon pauses outside the room for a moment, listening for any sound. He glances behind quickly. Then he returns his focus to the room. Jaydon dabs the door with his finger-tips. It moves a touch with the sound of a creek.

He peeps through the gap. Then clears the corners and enters. The room is lit in red. Summers has taped a black covering over the window.

He is quick to view contemporary black and white still life prints hung on a line, swaying in the air near a fan. Development trays, a sink, and an enlarger machine lay nearby. This is a photographic darkroom.

Jaydon inspects the hanging photos. There is a landscape, pebbles on a beach, a solitary tree, etc. Arty, but nothing unusual.

Jaydon looms over several images on a nearby desk. One particular picture catches his eye, which he takes a hold of for closer examination. He absorbs what he has just seen, places the photo in his pocket. then recomposes himself.

The detective hears a sound from the opposite room. Jaydon moves swiftly, but with caution. His pointed gun and torch continue to lead the way.

We are relieved by some natural light within this room. It is spartan. In fact, it is empty apart from a solitary wooden chair and a table placed at the centre, along with a collage on the far wall.

The collage contains photos and sheets, with various notes and scribbles. Smoke swirls above a glass ashtray left on the table, thanks to a smouldering half-used cigarette that continues to burn.

Jaydon swiftly strides to the open window and glances downwards towards the fire escape below. No one is there, but there was a moment ago.

He holsters his weapon and drifts forward to examine the collage more closely. His eyes dart back and forth intelligently, taking it all in.

Photographs of one man feature prominently on this board. He has black slicked-back hair and a narrow face. In some pictures, he wears dark sunglasses and is always well-dressed. A few photos have him with two burly men fitted into black suits over muscle, private protection.

Others show him entertaining a female companion at a restaurant and various coffee bars. The equation appears in the frame of each picture.

There are schedule lists with dates and some newspaper articles, one of which read, 'Suspected Weapons Smuggler Evades Conviction'. From the articles, Jaydon gathers this man's name, 'Gustavo Mayara'.

Jaydon reacts quickly to the sound of footsteps, gun aimed. Berg appears in the doorway, with his gun also pointed. They both relinquish their weapon. Berg views the surveillance whilst moving towards Jaydon and whistles.

Jaydon returns his attention to the collage. He spots an address written on scrap paper, which he rips from the wall. He rushes for the door, phone in hand.

'A possible crime in progress, 115 New Hope Street!'

23

WEDDING OR FUNERAL?

Cool modern soul plays in the background of yet another open-spaced contemporary apartment. Gustavo Mayara sits casually with his fiancée, Reina Heru.

The track's vocalist sounds similar to that of the famous musician, with the swept back hair and sultry voice from many decades ago. The vibe is super chilled.

Reina holds five wedding invitation designs. She sighs before spreading them on the light beige modern coffee table. Then scrutinises, 'What do you think?'

Gustavo, engrossed in his work, shows less attentiveness than his fiancée as he scans his iPad. He has seemingly not heard a word she has just said or attempted any aid with this very important dilemma. Reina glares at him incredulously. A hit on the shoulder gains his attention.

'Hey!' Gustavo says. He laughs whilst touching his shoulder and feigning outrage.

'This is important,' Reina says.

Gustavo raises his arms in defence. Then he places the device aside to provide his undivided attention. Reina points out the invitations on the table before them. Gustavo observes, scratching his head. 'I don't know. What do you think?'

'The ivory and silver one.'

Gustavo looks them over more closely, including the ivory and silver design, which indeed stands out from the pile. He considers this for a moment and then nods agreeably. 'It's sharp, contemporary. Yeah, I like it. Go for it.'

Gustavo sneaks Reina a glance as she sweeps up the cards. He then turns to her. 'But it doesn't matter what I think, does it? You're running the show.'

Reina smiles knowingly. 'That's not true.'

'Of course it is.' He moves in close. 'You made the choice days ago. Me saying yes just makes you feel better. The only thing you need from me is money to foot the bill.'

Reina hits him again, feigning mock outrage. He grabs both of her arms playfully and draws her in close. She laughs childishly.

'That's fine by me. All that matters is that this impeccable woman becomes my wife and eternal companion.' He lightly grazes her face with the back of his hand. 'I'm a changed man because of you.' *A changed man indeed.*

Actually, a radically transformed former criminal would be more accurate, as Gustavo was once a prominent international arms trafficker.

Africa served as his primary station—a seminal location for the illegal arms trade. There are multitudes of unoccupied land, and some parts of the continent are rife with corruption and a lax financial system.

He provided arms for militia groups operating in several conflict zones. Pistols, assault rifles, machine guns, explosives, and grenade launchers were all up for grabs on the black market.

Gustavo's cockiness led to his arrest when a bogus buyer lured him to the Philippines. Though he was not a fool and was well aware of the loopholes in national laws,

He never traded on UK territory, and none of his weapons reached British soil. The National Crime Agency was running out of cards to play. Gustavo knew this.

He made them an offer that was hard to refuse. He claimed he could provide the whereabouts of The Phantom if they dropped all charges against him and granted full immunity.

In the murky shores of criminal arms dealing, The Phantom was a whale. Anatoly Balabanov was a central figure in the clandestine engagement between Russia and the United States. The Russians were paramount in helping Iran develop their huge missile arsenal.

Topping the FBI's most wanted list with a four million-dollar bounty. Balabanov used several front companies based in Moscow to defraud United States banks, regulators, and customers. He had provided arms for over fifty percent of war-torn countries in some capacity over the last thirty years.

Balabanov evaded international laws through protection from The Mother Land. It also helped that he accumulated vast financial wealth and was extremely cautious.

Gustavo crossed paths with him once through a mutual acquaintance. He looked into this man's eyes and thought. *I don't know if there is a God, but I am certain that the devil exists*. His name was Anatoly Balabanov.

It cost several million to access the information that Anatoly owned a summer lake house somewhere in Canada. It cost a few more million for his address, but Gustavo was no fool. He knew that this information might be useful one day, and it was.

Finally, after nearly three decades of an arduous pursuit fraught with missteps and bogus leads, the FBI had their man. Authorities granted Gustavo immunity. Once again, he took advantage of national laws, holding some offshore assets.

Gustavo became a legitimate businessman with several digital companies. He met Reina a few years later and has never looked back.

Lost in the gaze of her emerald-coloured eyes. He thinks, *How lucky am I?*

Reina beams a smile made of pure joy. She rises from her seat, stretching out her tiredness, and moves to the window, admiring the moonlit sky. She pours herself a vintage glass of Pinot Noir. Then she turns to him, preparing her comeback.

There is a split-second flash of light from outside, which forms a spider crack in the window. Ksshhk! Reina drops to the floor like a heavy brick with a thud. A gunshot through the head!

Gustavo looks on in horror, overcome by shock. He remains wedged to the spot. Everything is going faster than his brain can cope with.

A 5.56mm bullet whizzes past his ear! Boom! Striking a nearby picture behind him, shattering glass.

Outside, there is a man approaching with a rifle. Gustavo ducks and crawls along the floor. He stops, now face to face with his beloved. Her vacant eyes stare into his as bullets rain hell from above.

24

THE SOLDIERS

Berg and Jaydon set their eyes steely on the road ahead, racing against time. The vehicle's siren wails in frustration, vocalising how Jaydon feels as they waste precious moments weaving through traffic.

Lights in skyscrapers, digital billboards, neon signs, and street lamps cause a radiant blur that reflects across the car's windows as they zoom through the nighttime city streets.

Jaydon's mind is drowning in thoughts, none of them positive. He just ended a call with a furious Gavin, which is rare. All because Jaydon entered Summers' apartment illegally and without backup.

✷ ✷ ✷

'Summers hasn't committed a crime yet. You had no right to enter his apartment!' Gavin said.

This frustrated Jaydon. 'What the hell's got into you?'

* * *

The truth of the matter is that Gavin is under extreme pressure right now from the higher-ups. The bizarreness of this case and the reinstatement of Jaydon are not helping.

Jaydon must toe the line. Gavin broke the rules in the past, both here and back home. It's a different time now. There is an intricacy at play, and a delicate balance is required.

* * *

Berg glances to the left as they near a crossroads. 'Clear!'

* * *

Jaydon rightfully argued that a man's life was in jeopardy. They were aware of this because of his actions.

* * *

There is also something else. He pushes that to the back of his mind and focuses on the road.

* * *

Gustavo is hiding in the oversized storage room through the slits of the louvre door. He views a man kitted out in full military attire holding an AR-15 semi-automatic rifle. Light-weight, air-cooled, gas-operated, and magazine-fed.

Gustavo traded quite a few in the past. How ironic he is to be killed with one. Gustavo recollects a time in Eastern Congo...

✻ ✻ ✻

He sat across the table from a hardened warlord in the midst of closing a business deal. Another member of the militia group occupied a corner.

The Warlord yelled for one of his child-soldiers. A boy in uniform, no older than thirteen, strode into the room. The Warlord pointed to the AR-15 on the table and commanded something in Swahili.

The child-soldier picked up the rifle and loaded the magazine. He pointed the weapon at the man in the corner, to his surprise, and shot him dead. The Warlord laughed heartily.

It turns out that this man was a traitor to the corrupt cause, providing vital strategic information to the enemy.

✻ ✻ ✻

Gustavo backs away cautiously and grabs a nearby wooden baseball bat. He listens out for his fate but hears nothing.

His heart breaks for Reina. This man is here to settle a debt for one of my past sins. *If it had been me standing at the window, maybe she'd still be alive.* His grip now tightens on the baseball bat. *Come and get some, you son of a bitch.*

Army boots tread against the parquet floor—the sound of the footsteps becoming louder as they approach: thump, thump, thump.

Jaydon and Berg skid to a stop outside Gustavo's home. They spring out of the vehicle and race to the house.

Jaydon spots an abandoned laptop nearby. As they approach, he notices that no force has been used to open the back door. Summers must have jammed the security system. He used the laptop and a portable radio frequency transceiver to overpower the central hub.

The footsteps stop. There is complete silence, apart from Summers' breath. The Bogeyman Soldier then turns toward the cupboard where Gustavo hides.

Jaydon is the first-man on entry. Up ahead is secure. He takes the blind spot, clearing the room. Berg moves forward close behind—gun at the ready.

Gustavo can feel Summer's energy permeating through the door. Footsteps shatter the silence: thump, thump, thump.

The cupboard door swings open. The backlight causes the soldier to appear in silhouette as he stands in the doorway. He points his weapon in Gustavo's direction.

'Police! Drop the weapon!'

Summers freezes. He lowers his aim from Gustavo but does not turn to face the two cops.

Jaydon stands further down the corridor. His SIG-Sauer P226 points directly at Summers—intensity radiating from his body. Berg is not far behind.

'Summers!' Berg warns. 'Do it now!'

Summers turns his head, but only slightly. He raises his weapon. Jaydon reacts like lightning. Bang! He shoots Summers in the leg, taking him down.

Summers has yet to let go of his gun. He glances upwards at Jaydon with a knowing smile, then swivels and takes aim. Bang, Bang! Double tap. Berg finishes the discussion.

Jaydon treads cautiously towards the soldier, who is down—still pointing his gun in Summers' direction. He kicks away the rifle.

Berg moves in. He kneels down and feels for a pulse. Then he shakes his head.

Jaydon holsters his weapon and sighs heavily. He tread reassuringly to Gustavo. 'I'm Detective Jaydon Lynch. Are you okay?'

• 25 •

MERCHANT OF DEATH

Flashing police and ambulance lights cut through Gustavo's window. Jaydon sits in a corner of the room, which is now a crime scene. He spots Berg, who lingers in the near distance, going over details with Gavin.

Berg removes his smartphone, presses the speed dial, and begins conversing with someone on the other end of the line. He glances over at Jaydon whilst drifting through the organised chaos, then moves out of sight.

Jaydon stands a few yards away from a dead Mark Summers in the adjacent room. The body of Reina Heru is another stiff, lying close by.

They have escorted Gustavo out of the building, and he is currently being looked after in King's Court. Jaydon is pondering what this man said to him...

'I'm Detective Jaydon Lynch. Are you okay?'

Gustavo Mayara looked up at Jaydon with bloodshot eyes and said, 'No, I'm not, Detective.' He gazed towards the soldier. 'That man is dead because of me. That beautiful, loving woman in the other room is dead because of me. They're not the only ones. I hazard to guess how much more.'

Gustavo contemplates. 'Tens of thousands? Hundreds of thousands? I was the merchant of death. It was foolish of me to think I could start a new life with so much blood on my hands.' He bowed his head in despair.

Soon after. A uniformed officer escorted him away.

✻ ✻ ✻

Gavin observes Jaydon, who sits in a corner across the room. He knows from experience that a police shooting is rare. The vast majority of officers spend decades on the force without this occurring. Gavin was not so fortunate.

✻ ✻ ✻

He shot and killed a nineteen-year-old back in Baltimore. The young man had a gun, which he fired. Gavin shot back. It was a justifiable shooting. This didn't make it any easier.

It always infuriated him when he watched those movies where the hero cop killed the bad guy, then mere moments later, acted like nothing ever happened.

He remembers one officer so traumatised by taking a life. He required eight months of therapy to come to terms with the enormity of the situation.

No cop he knew involved in a shooting forgot about it. Thought it was dope, or bragged.

✺ ✺ ✺

However, there was something unnerving about Berg. It didn't seem to affect him at all. *Water off a duck's back.*

Gavin treads wearily towards Jaydon. 'As you know, our man Gustavo escaped prosecution for his crimes. The law firm acting on Gustavo's behalf was Burling and Reed. Would you like to guess who his head counsel was?'

'Benjamin Colburn,' Jaydon says whilst he gazes off thoughtfully into the distance.

'That's correct.' Gavin appraises Jaydon for a moment. 'That was reckless; what you did earlier. This whole thing, I am not sure if Mark Summers was a perpetrator, a victim, or both, but if there were an arrest, the evidence would have been inadmissible in a court of law.'

'It's fortunate we shot him then.'

Gavin takes a deep breath. He then sits next to Jaydon, remaining calm. They observe Reina Heru's lifeless corpse as the coroner zips up the black body bag, ready to take her away.

'Forensics has your weapon. We will provide you with a replacement. Berg is already at the station making a statement. You need to follow suit. While there is an investigation pending, you'll be on administrative leave.'

Jaydon stands. 'How long for?'

'It was a righteous kill. It will be a short stint.'

'I can't do that. Not now.'

'Excuse me?'

Jaydon struggles to explain. 'I just can't.'

'Well, it's not up to you.'

'Gavin, you just have to trust me.'

Gavin rises from his seat. He looks Jaydon in the eyes. 'What the hell is this?'

Jaydon removes his phone. He speed-dials Caitlyn Colburn. It goes straight to the answering machine. 'After the beep, leave a message for Caitlyn.' The beep invites Jaydon to speak.

'Mrs Colburn, this is Detective Jaydon Lynch. You need to reach me on this number ASAP.' He ends the call.

'They're searching Summers' apartment as we speak. That's where our attention should be going. Mrs Colburn is off bounds via the rule of law.'

'I've seen everything I need to see there already.'

'Are you going to tell me what this is about?'

'Not yet.'

Gavin raises his hands in the air, and then looks up at the ceiling, searching for an answer. He then recomposes himself. 'You weren't the primary shooter. I guess I can hold them off until this is over.'

Jaydon nods. He then moves away and out of sight.

• 26 •

ROOM 145

On the drive over to Caitlyn's hotel, Jaydon once again ponders what she said to him. *Do you sometimes feel a void that only darkness can fill?*

Caitlyn is the only one left from this whole debacle. Jaydon is quite certain he identifies where this is going, but he has to be sure.

❋ ❋ ❋

Jaydon slows the unmarked vehicle to a halt outside the hotel. The detective pauses for a moment, then removes his seatbelt, exits the car and strides towards the building.

❋ ❋ ❋

Caitlyn's hotel room number reads '145'. Jaydon knocks on the door. 'Mrs Colburn?' He knocks again. There is no answer. Jaydon turns to leave, but he hears a continuous sound that is hard to decipher. *Running water, maybe?* He pauses a moment and knocks once more. No response. His instincts tell him *something is wrong*.

Jaydon assesses the room's door and spots that the dead latch switch is not fully engaged. He removes the privacy card from the door handle and feeds it through the gap near the bolt. There is a movement of the wrist that he applies with some finesse. The door clicks. The detective eases it open just enough to move through, then enters the space to examine.

Jaydon notices Caitlyn has left her bed ruffled and unkempt. He drifts past the large open window, where outside, a copious array of colourful city lights glisten in a bokeh soft blur.

The detective confirms that the noise was indeed running water, which trickles from the bathroom nearby. He moves heedfully towards the sound and stops at the entrance. 'Mrs Colburn? Caitlyn?'

The water continues to seep from under the door, which he knocks. There is no response apart from the flow of trickling liquid. Jaydon knocks again. The detective then dabs the door, which is not locked. He opens, filling the entrance.

He finds Caitlyn in a bath overflowing with water. She appears as though asleep. One arm lies limp on the side of the tub. She has cut both of her wrists.

The theory of committing suicide through a slit wrist in a bath tub aided by warm water is that it encourages the ease of blood flow, allowing for a painless way to depart whilst not leaving much of a mess behind.

This is a romanticised notion as it is extremely difficult to kill oneself in this way. To begin with, blood arteries lie fairly deep. A blood clot is a biological trigger that derives from blood vessels. This causes platelets to cluster at the location when attempting to seal the wound. Water might slow this down, but it won't hinder it completely. This is fortunate for Caitlyn.

Jaydon lifts her flaccid body out of the water, which splashes at his feet and all over the tiled floor. He lowers her to the ground and finds several nearby towels, hastily binding them tightly around her wrist.

He carries Caitlyn out of her room to the lift. Then from the lift towards the hotel entrance, causing shock and horror for the serving staff and guests that locate the lobby. Then, finally, to his vehicle.

Jaydon burns down the street towards the Central City Hospital. Caitlyn lies near to unconscious in the passenger seat. He turns to her. Brushing strands of wet hair from her face with his fingers. 'Stay with me.'

He considers the thoughts and emotions that must have flooded her mind leading up to this point. Guilt, pain, despair. The worry of losing her children. Her life ruined.

Jaydon concludes. The true Caitlyn did not prevail on that fateful morning when she shot her husband. *She is paying the price for the actions of her shadow side.*

Jaydon stops the car outside the hospital. With a burst of energy, he springs out of his seat and dashes around to the passenger side, promptly opening the door and delicately raising her up into his embrace.

He rushes to the hospital entrance, in which the automated doors part on his approach. A panting Jaydon, with Caitlyn heavy in his arms, hastens towards the ER's reception. 'Somebody help! I need some help here!'

• 27 •

BLOOD AND WATER

The last thing I remembered was being enveloped in warm water. I lay in the bath and relaxed as my life faded away. A merciful relief from the misery of my current existence.

❊ ❊ ❊

I regain consciousness for a moment. Detective Jaydon Lynch is crouching over me whilst tying each of my wrists with a towel.

❊ ❊ ❊

A short while before, I sat in my room and spoke to Lyle over the phone. I heard the words, 'temporary insanity plea,' and, 'a good chance of an acquittal,' but my mind was elsewhere...

❊ ❊ ❊

It was the day Mia was born. She was a healthy baby, that wouldn't stop crying. I could never understand why she wouldn't stop crying.

Benjamin had made junior partner at Burling and Reed. The man I married was morphing into another person. 'We can't pay for a mortgage on ideals alone.'

Benjamin provided lead defence for a famous film producer accused of raping several young women. He tore apart one accuser in court. The jury found the defendant not guilty. The film producer walked free.

My mother, Celia, was an English professor and a rape victim. The perpetrator was one of her colleagues. She pressed charges but experienced bullying and harassment during the interview process.

They later dismissed the charges because of claims of inconsistency in her statement. The polices response to rape victims was appalling back then.

I watched my mother suffer through anxiety, mood swings, helplessness, and social withdrawal during this period. My father and I attended to the needs of my younger sister. I was just eleven years old.

Once again, I regain consciousness. I am in the detective's car. Unlike the warm bath, my hands and feet are like ice. I feel lightheaded...

* * *

Tensions brewed between me and Benjamin—late one night. We got into a heated argument whilst driving home from a restaurant.

A word of advice. Don't burn down a narrow, winding country road at 80mph when distracted. You may lose control and hit a tree.

I suffered a distal radial fracture, a broken leg, and a bruised spleen. Benjamin, who was driving, miraculously escaped with just a sprained wrist and a few cuts and bruises.

The first night in the hospital, Benjamin didn't leave my bedside. Through my hazy, morphine fuelled gaze, I glimpsed the man I had once married.

I heard the words, 'legal aid,' 'rectifying mistakes,' 'starting our own law firm together,' and 'seeking justice once more,' before the drugs took me into a peaceful black.

Peaceful black. That is where I was heading before the detective came along. I am in his arms. He moves towards the hospital reception. A nurse approaches. *Why do I feel so connected to this man?*

I ended the call with Lyle. Then, anguished at the unspeakable horror I have brought upon my poor children.

I ran the bath. Then retrieved the chef's knife I bought earlier. I did not bother to remove my clothing when I entered the bath. I lay there, after slicing my wrist, and drifted away. The soothing water diluted the redness of the blood. My thoughts washed over me...

* * *

My husband stood by his words to a degree. He worked pro-bono with clients who needed his help in The Slums.

We never started our own firm, though. Benjamin remained at Burling and Reed, as he was already a Senior Partner.

During an extended family holiday in Singapore, my mother confided in me about her former ordeal. It had been many years. 'I would not have been able to heal without you and your father.'

* * *

I hear the sounds of beeping machines, medical jargon, and clattering wheels. Less muffled as my eyes flicker open to a blur of images upon white. A ceiling dotted with fluorescent lights whips past in a haze. They wheel me along on a gurney.

My eyes find the detective alongside flustered doctors and nurses. They peer down at me. I graze his arm with my hand. The doctors and nurses push the detective aside. He becomes smaller as the gurney speeds away.

*** *** ***

My eyes slowly open, blinking in the light above. The figures at a distance are thin silhouettes in a Gaussian blur. It is as if they are not human but alien. The aliens melt away. My eyes close.

FATHERS AND DAUGHTERS

The reception clock reads *2:47 a.m.* It is an eerily quiet midweek early morning in the ER.

Jaydon is privy to the scene, which takes place through the open blinds of the white clinical A+E recovery room's window.

Caitlyn lies sedated. It has been six hours since the suicide attempt. Her younger sister, Sara Girard, son Zachary Colburn, and his girlfriend, Kasuko Himura, surround her. Dr Howard provides care.

'You're still here.'

Jaydon turns to the voice that has entered his space. Mia Colburn approaches. She slows to a stop outside the window. Mia holds a branded, reusable cup filled with coffee. She blows, then takes a sip. Her eyes are red.

'Hi, Mia, right?'

Mia nods in confirmation. Now a spectator of the unfortunate scene taking place through the blind-filled window. 'I've been here the whole time, but just wasn't able to...' Mia takes a deep breath. 'I guess I should thank you.'

'Just doing my job.'

Mia appraises Jaydon. *He doesn't look like the usual cop.* 'My friends who live in The Slums don't trust the police.'

Jaydon offers a tired half smile. 'Then me and your friends have something in common.'

'What kind of policeman are you?'

'I'm the one who catches the bad guys no one else can catch.'

She observes Jaydon with curiosity. 'Is that how you got your scar, doing your work?'

'You certainly ask a lot of questions.'

'I'm naturally inquisitive.'

Jaydon nods to himself. 'I have, had a daughter almost your age... We all have scars, I guess.'

Had? She senses the tragedy and wonders how it occurred. There is an awkward silence. A father without a daughter. A daughter without a father.

Mia is awash with emotions. The fear of losing her mother accompanies the hatred of what she has done. There is shame, as she recalls the lingering eyes of people at college, who offer glances and whispers.

Her mind churns. She has to understand. *Is my mother insane like people are saying?* 'Why did she do it?'

'Most likely guilt for what she felt she did to your father and you and your brother.'

'No, I mean, why did she kill him?'

Jaydon pauses a moment before speaking. 'Honestly, I can't say for sure. But what I know is when someone kills, it leaves a mark. No matter how hard they try to bury it, to hide it away. It's always there, deep within their very soul. I see a lot of things when I look at your mother. I don't see that.'

A voice calls. 'Mia'

Sara stands outside the entrance. Her arms are out-stretched. Mia's eyes linger on Jaydon for a few moments before she meanders a few paces to her aunt. Sara hugs her niece warmly. She keeps an arm around Mia's shoulder and escorts her to the entrance of Caitlyn's room.

Mia's gaze once again finds Jaydon, and in that moment, she thinks, *what now?* This is a predicament that you truly cannot prepare for.

She stands at the doorway, watching her mother sleep, feeling trepidation. Unsure whether to take one step forward or three back.

The Doctor draws the blinds shut as Mia enters the room. Jaydon is privy no more.

• 29 •

ER

Dr Rebecca Howard treads down the hospital corridor. It's time for a caffeine boost. She truly loves her job but admits it is not for the faint of heart.

She observes the ER, which is eerily quiet for this time of night, even for mid-week. Apart from Mrs Colburn, there has been very little action.

She offered to do this shift, which was better than the alternative—home, in front of the TV, with a bad reality show on display, whilst her thoughts rested upon Isaiah and what transpired.

The ER is a place where the beeping monitors offer background ambience to patients in distress. This might be moaning, crying, swearing, shouting, or those suffering in silence.

Who or how many will come through that door is unpredictable, but they will arrive. It may be by ambulance, by car, or simply dropped at the entrance like a parcel.

For every generic knife-wound, heart attack, or those being seen for minor inflictions or illness, there is always something a little less conventional.

Patients with items lodged in a part of their body it most definitely shouldn't be, or vice versa. Individuals being impaled, those pronounced dead, brought back to life or the dam right psychotic.

She smiles to herself. *Bring it on.*

There are spaces for silence. A vacant unit. The staff room, or Isaiah's favourite location, the chapel.

Up ahead, she spots the detective purchasing coffee from a vending machine. This man certainly has a habit of showing up in the wrong place at the right time.

'No home to go to, Doctor?'

'I took a double shift. I'm more useful here than... Anyway, I work here. What's your excuse?'

'I'm hoping to speak to Mrs Colburn.'

'That's not possible. At least for a few more days.'

Jaydon nods in understanding.

Dr Howard searches the pockets of her green scrubs, retrieving a wallet phone case, then purchases an espresso from a coffee machine. She presses buttons and scans her card on the neighbouring machine. The oats bar she requests doesn't quite make it, stuck in limbo.

She breathes out a deep sigh. Jaydon moves in and pushes the machine. The snack falls. He retrieves it and hands it to her. Their eyes meet for a moment. Weary understanding passes between them. 'Thanks.'

Dr Howard remains certain Isaiah was not himself. *How could he be?* Now, a second suicide attempt. This woman, Caitlyn Colburn, was unsuccessful, whereas Isaiah succeeded. The same police officer. *This is not a coincidence.*

When they questioned her following Isaiah's passing, the police were reluctant to divulge much information. Something else is going on here. *Why search for Isaiah in the first place? Are there more people behind this?* Her instincts tell her she should disclose what she has learnt.

'You know, Caitlyn was lucky. She was involved in a car accident roughly two years ago. They conducted physio and psychotherapy here. We had access to all of her medical records. It saved her life.'

The detective's eyes widen. Rebecca sees the cogs churning in his mind.

'Therapy. Dr Howard. I need access to your database right now.'

. *.* *.*

Dr Howard stands behind the reception desk. Jaydon is nearby. She gathers information from a computer. The detective mentioned that someone might have manipulated several people, which included Caitlyn and Isaiah. She is eager to help.

'You are right; each of the people you mentioned spent time in an A+E in the last few years.' She continues to type...

'All hospitals in the country have interconnected databases. Unless they spent time here, we need a release form to access their full medical records. Like what we had for Mrs Colburn.'

The detective ponders for a moment. 'Do you have doctors who may be required to work in multiple hospitals? For instance, a therapist specialising in a particular field?'

'No, it doesn't work that way, unless...' She types some more.

'Wait, because they all had traumatic experiences, each hospital assigned them a psychotherapist. What are the odds? It's the same person. His main office is in the city. The work he does here is pro bono.'

Jaydon nods knowingly to himself. 'Oz.'

'Pardon me?'

He turns to Dr Howard with a crooked smile. 'What's his name?'

'Cain, Jeremiah Cain.'

• 30 •

THE ORGANISATION

Reports of telepathic experiments in Russia date back to the late nineteenth century. The Russian Science for Experimental Psychology, founded in 1891, held an interest in psychometry, clairvoyance, and hypnotism, amongst other things.

Their scientist conducted countless ESP and telepathy studies under Stalin's regime. The parapsychologists in Leningrad actively manipulated consciousness through telepathy, and their EEG recordings provided encouragement.

Some say the Doctors were doing this for theoretical reasons, with the aim of mathematically proving the possibility of an electromagnetic carrier of telepathy. It would be enhanced in a manner similar to radio waves and propagated through society and culture via influencers.

Since the early twentieth century, the Soviets had explored and perfected all the advantages that hypnotism could provide. Entangled within a web of espionage, the post-hypnotic suggestion was used to steal classified documents denoting important military equipment alongside other clandestine operations, all without the persons having knowledge of what they had done.

Russian scientists made significant efforts to manipulate individuals to suit their needs. Working with the drugs Mescaline and Psilocybin in combination with psychic tests.

During the early period of the Cold War, the CIA became convinced that the Soviets had discovered drugs and techniques that could allow them to control the human mind. They began their own programme, MK-ultra, in response.

Alongside telepathic hypnosis, the employees within MK-Ultra conducted experiments with LSD on mental patients, prisoners, drug addicts, and prostitutes. They also administered LSD to CIA employees, military personnel, doctors, and members of the public.

One aim was to find drugs that could expose any hidden confessions. The other was to wipe the subject's mind clean for reprogramming.

Additional MK-Ultra drug-related experiments involved Heroin, Morphine, Temazepam Mescaline, Psilocybin, Scopolamine, Alcohol, and Sodium Pentothal. The experiments continued until the programmes ended in 1972.

This is what they tell you. This is what the New Global Organisation would like you to think. However, the results derived from the MK-Ultra experiments were too important to be thrown away.

The New Global Organisation. Let's call them The Organisation for short, are a cabal of elites with dominant political and economic power. They proliferate every facet of international government, media, financial and educational institutions, and culture. The power behind the powerful. They are watching, profiting, and influencing.

The Organisation absorbed a splinter group of MK-Ultra and hired me as a private contractor, tolerating my experiments with the human condition as a silly little side project due to my importance.

I let them believe they own me, abiding by their demands when needed. Moving in the shadows, influencing the influencers, and whispering orders in the guise of suggestions for puppet leaders to follow. Though never forgetting my ultimate purpose. To unveil humanity's true face.

You could call me an agent of free will. Something more prescient. Maybe just for now, call me Jeremiah Cain.

• 31 •

THE THERAPIST

Berg, Jaydon and Gavin hurry through The King's Court's corridor towards the exit of the station. 'The equation homicides are intimate and personal. He knew these people, their fears, desires, and hopes. How so?' Jaydon asks.

✳ ✳ ✳

Jeremiah Cain sits in his office. It is sparse and modern. A blue and green abstract painting offers colour amongst a predominantly white and chrome palette.

Various journals and psychology books lay neatly on the metal shelf pinned to the wall. A metronome sits on his glass desk nearby. Its pendulum rocking from side to side, ticking like a clock.

Elaine Short, a young woman dressed in office attire, with black hair, pale skin, and red lipstick, reclines on the white couch. She gazes distantly at the wall ahead whilst the psychotherapist sits a short distance away, cross-legged, listening and scribbling occasional notes. The atmosphere in the room lingers with a slight edge.

'I have this reoccurring dream. Stuck in this black hole, a deep bottomless pit. I'm being dragged further and further down by these faceless wraiths and shadows. The more I struggle, the deeper they pull me in. I can't breathe.'

Elaine feels slightly hesitant, knowing this reoccurring dream may be the key to uncovering the root cause of her psychological issues. *Am I sure about this?* She pauses uneasily, waiting for confirmation to continue.

Cain adjusts in his seat. Then, he smiles a smile that doesn't quite reach his eyes. 'It's okay.'

'I try to scream, but there's no sound. I look up, and I am at the edge. Staring down with a blank expression as I fall.'

'The reoccurring dream often suggests something significant is being overlooked. During our time in these sessions, we will try to bring to light what has been buried deep in the unconscious.'

* * *

'Because he holds a position of trust,' Gavin says. They jog towards their vehicles.

'I don't understand,' Berg says.

'Some kind of counsellor or psychotherapist,' Gavin says.

'Not just any psychotherapist. Someone who specialises in hypnotic suggestion and trauma therapy.'

'You've narrowed it down.'

'To one,' Jaydon says.

Gavin opens the unmarked vehicle's driver's side door and hurriedly gets inside. Jaydon moves to the vehicle's passenger side and then makes his way in. Berg enters the back seat—the car engine revs before zooming down the city street towards Cain's office.

Cain sits perfectly still at his desk. He chose this office for its wonderful view of the city skyline, particularly at night.

Cain is currently admiring the view at this very moment. So, as Gavin and Jaydon enter his office, they find him with his back turned.

He senses their presence and wonders *what the final solution to this equation will be, now that all the pieces are in place?*

Cain opened the door to his office. It was nighttime. The only form of luminance was the glimmering city lights outside his window and a switched-on desk lamp. He had a visitor. Guess who...?

Doll Face remained hidden in shadow. 'You don't seem surprised to see me.'

'I'm not.'

Cain threw a newspaper on the desk. It contained the same headline as what was on Jaydon's digital newspaper device when called by the killer. He stared at the monster with utter contempt and waited for a response.

'He was getting too close.'

Cain strolled to the window. He admired the view. *Stick to the plan.* 'The police are going to turnover this entire city looking for you.'

'I know how they work.'

He felt the eyes of the monster bore through the back of his neck. 'You're such a hypocrite. You look at me like scum. I hear nothing but disdain in your voice when you speak to me.'

Cain turned. He moved in with purpose. 'Who do you think you're talking to? You are an ant standing in the presence of a giant.

'Just remember, you would be nothing but a scared little boy without me. My opinion of you means nothing in the larger scale of things.'

Cain then sat and relaxed in a chair opposite the shadowed man. 'Besides, I have a plan. A plan that entails an intricate form of events leading to you right at the centre. Something so incredible. There will be no words to describe it. Are you willing to make the sacrifice?'

'What kind of sacrifice?'

'The ultimate kind.'

Cain felt the change in Doll Face's countenance. A heightening of adrenaline mixed with excitement.

'Yes. Yes, I am.'

'Good. When you return home, I want you to make a phone call.'

* * *

Cain sits perfectly still at his desk. His back remains turned. Jaydon and Gavin move in—as the metronome ticks. 'Detectives, I've been waiting for you.'

• 32 •

SHADOWS ON A WALL

Detective Jaydon Lynch and the psychotherapist face each other from across the table. An overhead lamp is the only source of luminance. It's all somehow befitting for this showdown.

* * *

Gavin and Berg stand in the adjoining room, parted by the one-way mirror, watching it all play out. It's tense.

* * *

Jaydon profiles this man, who is half-lit. A shadow falls across his face. Cain has displayed a mixture of calm self-assurance, arrogance, and ego. He was extremely cool and at ease when they strode into his office this morning to make the arrest.

The detective infers that the psychiatrist had conceived everything meticulously up until now, and nothing would have changed. He is here because he wants to be. *This is all part of the plan.*

Jaydon holds a folder containing pictures of a scrapbook. 'We had a good look around your home and office. Gathered some interesting information, including this.'

He then slides the open folder towards Cain. The pictures of the scrapbook show pages that contain more of Saravanan Vishwakarma's work. 'Saravanan Vishwakarma's summations, I assume, were more of an inspiration?'

'You could say that.'

'It must have taken some considerable time and effort to plan something so meticulously. We experienced the when and the where.' He then pauses for a moment and ponders. 'Now, the how? I think I have that figured out. Was it post-telepathic hypnosis? I would guess a combination of words spoken over the phone that created a trigger.'

'The how is not what you should be asking. What you should be more curious about is the why. It is time that we, as a species, come to terms with who we are.'

Cain moves completely into the light. 'How does it make you feel, knowing this so-called civilised society is just a trick? A simple illusion, like shadows on a wall.'

'Maybe I don't see it that way.'

'Well, you should. Do you really believe in it all? Civilisation. Mankind. For a selected few to lead, and without question, the herd will blindly follow.

machine guns they had, await them, secure in the vehicle outside.

Avery appraises his partner, sensing something is off. 'What's going on?'

Owens looks up and shakes his head. We have carried out all the close-quarter combat and advanced firearms preparation. *So, why am I still nervous?* 'Have you wondered why they are doing this? I mean, I get it. Where we are going now is not great, but...'

Avery moves to his partner and takes a seat beside him. 'I remember when you were a wet behind the ear's rookie. I thought that kid would never make it through recruitment. Boy, was I wrong?'

He places a hand on the younger man's shoulder. 'I have had several partners in my career. I can say without a doubt, there is no one I trust out there more to have my back.' He refers to the gun. 'This thing, think of it as a deterrent rather than something to cause harm.'

'It could amplify things, though, right? Every day, we protect and serve while risking our lives. For what? Terrible pay and a blanket call for our heads the moment one of us makes a mistake. No matter how much good the rest of us do.'

'I do this because it's my calling. Try to care less about what other people think and focus more on the job.'

Owens nods his head. The two men then ready themselves to move into The Slums.

'The fundamental problem is, human beings aren't sheep. They're a different kind of animal. Only as civilised as they have to be, as they're made to be. Take the boundaries away, and you'll see. I'll show you. Rules, laws, social order, all thrown out the window.'

'I don't think so.'

'Stop lying, Detective. You, yourself, are not one to shy away from breaking the rules.'

'I did what I had to.'

'Yes, you did. Why shouldn't you? A Hoodlum, backed into a corner, guns down three rival gang members, whilst a soldier, stranded behind enemy lines, holds off his captors, killing several men. One is a hero, and the other is a villain. Who decides what we should perceive as being just? To deny our basic instincts is to deny ourselves.'

'Maybe so, but I still hold the belief that people are inherently good.'

The psychiatrist pauses for a moment. His interest is piqued. He analyses Jaydon but says nothing.

'The simple fact of the matter is that you manipulated those people. Twisting their minds to prove some sick theory, that's all.'

'I didn't force anyone to do what they did. I just opened the door. They're the ones who walked through it.'

With a knock, Berg pops his head around the half-open door. 'DCI Lynch.'

Cain now recedes into full shadow. 'You're aware that the last few pieces of the puzzle are still to be solved?'

Jaydon retrieves the folder containing the pictures and holds it aloof. 'Yes, and for your part, I believe I just have. Making an arrest plus evidence, equals jail.'

He stops a recording device, rises from his seat, and moves towards the door.

Berg peers curiously over Jaydon's shoulder towards Cain, whose energy remains transfixed as they move away. Berg slams the door shut, following Jaydon's exit—the sound echoing off the concrete walls in the hollow space.

• 33 •

CAIN OR NOT CAIN?

Recently approved firearms officer, Finn Owens, sits tensely on The Central Municipal Police Station changing room bench. John Avery, his senior partner, stands nearby at a locker. They are both kitted in bullet-proof vests.

Avery tools up with a newly minted Glock 17 handgun, courtesy of this dammed initiative scheme, constantly reported and debated on television. He throws some possessions into his locker and slams the door shut.

Owens holds his gun lightly in his grasp. He observes the weapon and contemplates. *Heavier than it looks.* This is one of only a handful of occasions that he has held a weapon since training. The first time was when the higher-ups requested they assist DSI Gavin Reece, whilst pursuing the suspect, Isaiah Carpenter.

DSI Reece was unaware that firearm officers would be on the scene. *The higher ups had no right going behind the DSI's back.*

To be honest, he was relieved when the chief ordered them to stay put. The Heckler & Koch MP5 carbine sub-

CPS prosecutor, Dominic Remel, stands in the dark. He observes the psychiatrist through the one-way glass, where the interview room is now fully lit. Cain sips tea with a polystyrene cup in hand as if at home on a Sunday afternoon.

Gavin hastily enters. Jaydon and Berg follow. Jaydon carries the look of a confused man. 'Do you want to run that by me again?'

'We performed a biometrics check with previous data as a precaution. It's not a match. In fact, there is no match. Whoever this man is, It's not the psychiatrist, Jeremiah Cain,' Gavin says.

'I don't understand,' Dominic says.

'The check was thorough. Jeremiah Cain graduated twenty years ago. He completed his residency at St Mary's Hospital four years later. Then, he fell off the grid and vanished in a ball of smoke, nothing.

'Someone appears a decade later with all of Cain's credentials: birth certificate, medical license, the works.

'He then proceeds to open his own practice. The person I am referring to is that man right there.' Gavin points to the False-Cain through the one-way view. Who, as if on cue, looks upwards in their direction, his eyes piercing.

'Gavin, the guy's been doing this for years, working with experts and publishing journals. Are you sure about this?' Jaydon asks.

'We have employee biometrics data going back years. The real Cains information synchs with dental and DNA. The genetic information for the Cain you are looking at does not.'

'How is this even possible?'

'I have no idea, but as of now, we might as well be viewing a ghost.'

Dominic scans the faces of the people in the room around him for further explanation. There is none. Hands raised to hips, he shakes his head in disbelief. 'Unbelievable!'

• 34 •

KERFUFFLE

Rage fills Yasiel Caddel. He strides towards Baxter's Café. That's where Big Man will be. He snorts in contempt. Big Man is how they refer to him.

Bathed in red, blue, and yellow neon lights from an off-licence and the few shops that remain open. Yasiel moves past a group of hoodlums lurking in a dark corner.

Further along, he ignores the pleas from several homeless people loitering on the pavement, finding shelter under one of a number of derelict buildings.

Yasiel has lived here all his life, deciding to stay when he could have left years ago. He wonders, *is fighting for the soul of this area a lost cause.*

A couple of miles from here is Angel Square, where the destitute suffer in discord. Tents pitched near fire bins as junkies meander around aimlessly. This part of the area encompasses a unique smell of burning litter mixed with alcohol, urine, vomit, and faeces.

Welcome to Kendersford, ladies and gentlemen. The vertex within the trilateral, labelled The Slums. Up ahead, he spots Big Man's cronies stationed outside the café.

Yasiel's work involves helping young people from broken homes. For every success, there are several failures.

He's aware that structure begins in the home, with additional help from the community. When this breaks down, everything around it collapses.

He aimed to highlight this whilst appearing on the radio podcast the other day. Though, his fellow guest Godfrey Mann had a point. What did he say? *Let's not pretend we don't know the individuals responsible for poisoning this region and corrupting the youths.* He was right.

Yasiel has been mentoring Naomi for the last two years. A seventeen-year-old student way ahead of her peers, extremely rare for someone of her background. They found the narcotic Pops in her possession at her college. She was dealing.

That's how it starts. Then, they graduate to the even harder stuff whilst shifting more of a supply. He had to beg, plead, and call in several favours for her to avoid being booted out or arrested.

Naomi wouldn't have been in contact with Big Man directly, but it doesn't matter. *We still need to speak.*

Yasiel approaches the thugs stationed outside the café, who get in his face. He moves past them and enters to the sound of a jangling bell and the stony gaze of Big Man's right-hand man, Rusty 'Chuckles' Dyson. Chuckles doesn't offer a smile. He never does. 'What you doing here?'

Chuckles and Yasiel have had beef in the past. Whilst Yasiel worked tirelessly for youngsters in the community, adamant they stayed clear of anything to do with drugs. Chuckles actively recruited the youths for drug dealing.

Yasiel locks eyes with Chuckles. He recalls a time when he risked his life to get a kid out, but not just any kid. This was family...

* * *

One mid-summer night, his older sister Deborah phoned him in hysterics. She was anxious about her fourteen-year-old son, who had not come home for two days.

Calvin was being held up in The Factory. This was the name of the den where they gathered the drug supplies and daily earnings.

Yasiel miraculously rescued the boy and escaped with his life. There was a tense ordeal with Chuckles, who said, 'It's only because of the Big Man that I haven't put you in the ground.' Calvin has recently enrolled in university and is doing well.

* * *

A voice from behind several hoodlums speaks. Tinted with regional accent and street slang. 'Blood, relax-up. Let the man pass through.' Chuckles and the other thugs in Yasiel's purview step aside to reveal Kojo Little. The thirty-three-year-old gang boss sits at a table, fingers enclosed around a cup of coffee.

Yasiel moves towards Kojo but does not take a seat. 'We need to speak outside bruv.'

Kojo and Yasiel exit the café. The boss delivers an order to the thugs loitering outside. 'Bounce.' The hoodlums hastily stagger down the street.

Yasiel appraises Kojo, whose face has hardened. It has been close to a year since he last saw him and another several months before then.

They were inseparable whilst growing up, watching each other's back and fighting just to survive.

Then, the children became teenagers. The teenagers became adults. That's where their paths diverged.

'They found one of my kids selling Pops bruv.'

'That's not my problem, blood.'

'You are the only supplier around here.'

'How old was the youth?'

'Seventeen.'

'Old enough to make choices on road.'

'Like the choices you made.'

'What choices do you think those are?'

'Spreading this filth around the neighbourhood.'

Kojo smiles and shakes his head.

'What's so funny?'

'The drugs will find their way here, no matter what. That's what the rich peopledem want. I don't play by their rules.

'Sure, I sell a little here and there on road. The main bulk of my supply goes to the elites, blood. Politicians, tycoons, actors, socialites, singers, their friends. They like to party and pay well for a good time.

'There are groups planning to tear this place down and rebuild. That's why we're all up in the media. To create tension so they can act.

'I'm gonna invest. They don't care about us, but things will turn around quickly once the wealthy peopledem move in. That's how we help, you get me.'

'Like you're helping the community now?'

'I'm not the problem? Just a symptom. Open your eyes, blood—the ones doing the actual damage. The real cartels are the pharmaceutical companies, helped by the media. Selling drugs for depression they caused, and illnesses that we don't have, making legit bank. Billions.'

A kid by the name of Justin approaches. This young person is on the community programme and happens to be under Yasiel's supervision.

If you hold Naomi as an example of someone smart and capable who has worked hard for a chance to beat the odds, then view Justin as the exact opposite.

'Tell yourself what you need to, bruv. Just stay clear of my youths.' Yasiel moves to the kid. He grabs him and searches his pockets to find a huge wad of cash. 'What's this?!'

Justin then snatches the cash back. 'You're not my dad. You can't tell me what to do!'

Chuckles and the crew spot the kid and Yasiel. 'I told that youth to go straight to the factory after earning on road. Why is Justin here, near us and Big Man?'

What they haven't spotted is a vehicle parked a little further up—a marked police car.

* * *

Avery and Owens monitor the kerfuffle outside Baxter's Café. They recognise a few of Kojo Little's crew. The National Drug Unit have been trying to nail him for a couple of years, but he keeps slipping through their fingers.

* * *

Chuckles rushes outside the entrance and launches into Yasiel with punches and kicks. Big Man's thugs are ready to join in. Fourteen-year-old Justin finds himself caught in the middle. Kojo is nowhere to be seen.

'Pack it in!' Avery barks from a distance. The thugs wise up and back away.

Yasiel and Chuckles either ignore the cops or are oblivious. They unleash years of pent-up disdain as they roll on the ground, fighting. Justin, the stupid boy caught up in emotions, pulls out a knife and viciously stabs Yasiel several times.

A gunshot puts an end to the whole thing and also the kid's life. He lies on the street in a pool of blood.

• 35 •

DELIRIUM

In the adjoining room, Jaydon moves towards the one-way mirror. He scrutinises the man sitting on the other side.

The man that he is analysing returns the stare. His eyes are like lasers burning through the one-way glass, which he supposedly cannot see through.

'He said it wasn't over. Did you manage to get a hold of his other patients?'

'Most of them,' Berg says. Head buried in an open folder filled with files. He turns and leaves.

What this man has done is literally unheard of. *How did he manage it all?* Jaydon knows he would not have gained access to forged ID on his own. W*ho helped him?* Yet, there is something else that the detective can confirm. *I'm the last piece.*

* * *

Avery moves towards Justin with purpose. He directs his gun at the limp body lying on the pavement. The firearms officer kicks away the weapon and kneels in close. His fingers finding the side of the kid's neck, searching for a pulse, but there's none.

'Jesus John?' Owens says.

Avery begins administering CPR. Owens moves to their vehicle and grabs his CB radio, which crackles.

'Sierra Oscar 5, this is Officer Owens requesting an ambulance and all available units to Halifax Street, Kendersford. We have an officer involved shooting—the kid. I mean, the assailant is down. There has also been a stabbing. Over.'

The voice that emanates from the CB radio crackles with a reply. 'Received.'

Chuckles stares down at the kid on the pavement. He makes a beeline for Avery. Owens steps in front of him, pointing his gun. Stopping the big guy mid-stride. 'Back away!'

* * *

The moment Kojo spotted the yellow, blue, and black police car, an internal voice said, *bounce*.

Not because of any apprehensions that the fuzz would stroll in and arrest him. No, he's the Big Man, a high-roller who has remained separate from any visible dealings for quite a while.

His major worries revolve around the plants that the elites have installed. Instigators of chaos, with the sole purpose of stirring things up and piggybacking off of genuine concerns within the community to create havoc and destroy.

The powerful would then swoop in and rebuild from the rubble, evicting a good portion of the locals to construct their vision. They have told him this.

Each time he spots police that are packing, he is alert. One incident is all they require.

Murder, gang wars, kidnapping. He's done it all. Kojo has managed to keep his head above water through intelligence and instincts. Now, it's time to leave this life behind.

He meant what he said to Yasiel. He wants to become a bank. A legit Big Man. Why not also help the community where he grew up? The ones who remain, that is.

Kojo hears police sirens, *or is it an ambulance*? He removes the hood from his head, moves to his car, opens the door, and enters. Kojo drives away to his luxurious three-million-pound apartment in the centre of the megalopolis.

✻ ✻ ✻

Chuckles stands firm. He locks eyes with Owens in a standoff. Avery wipes away the perspiration from his forehead. He points his gun in Chuckle's direction whilst standing. 'He said back off!'

Chuckles maintains eye contact with Owens whilst he slowly retreats. Avery returns to his knees and continues CPR on Justin.

Yasiel lies on his back, holding several knife wounds to his side. He glances sideways at the police and the dead child and feels sadness. Owens treads towards him and kneels down. 'Sir, help is on its way.'

This young cop looks nervous, Yasiel thinks.

Owens shuffles anxiously, his eyes bouncing. The neighbourhood has caught wind of the whole situation. Flashing lights of the marked vehicle are not doing much to help their cause. Shadows loom in the darkness. They switch on bedroom lamps. Curtains shift.

Chuckles vanishes into the night for a moment. Then he returns with a gunmetal grey rubbish bin that he hurtles towards the windscreen of the police car, forming a large spider web of glass.

The looming shadows move in for the kill. Some shout in protest, whilst others, looking to create chaos, holler with encouragement. These are all the ingredients needed for a riot, ladies and gentlemen.

• 36 •

NO ONE IS IMMUNE

Dominic, Jaydon, and Gavin each hold a corner. They deliberate on the events that have taken place. The main point of contention being the man whose real name is unknown at the centre of it all. Let's continue calling him Cain. Currently being transferred to the Central Municipal Police Station.

'What are you trying to say here?' Dominic asks.

'It is pretty obvious, is it not? He coerced and manipulated these people,' Jaydon says.

'That would be difficult to prove in a court of law.'

'He had personal one-on-one time with each of the suspects. He instigated all of this. Christ, he just more or less admitted it!'

'Who is he exactly? We don't even know who this man is. Right now, we have him on identity fraud. The little evidence I have examined is compelling. Let's see where the rest of this leads us.'

'What about Caitlyn?'

'What about her?'

'You are going to work something out, right?'

'We won't decide how to go about this until we complete discovery.'

'She's not a murderer.'

'Well, she's something. Anyway, how can you be so sure that some part of her didn't want to do this?'

Jaydon replays Caitlyn's words in his mind. *Do you sometimes feel a void that only darkness can fill?* When it boils down to our shadow side. *No one is immune.* He shakes his head at the internal dialogue.

Dominic rises and moves towards Jaydon. His mien softens. 'We will make an impartial decision about what charges to file after studying all the evidence. Who knows, we might come to the same conclusions you have.'

As the Lawyer moves to the door. Gavin asks, 'You never explained why your superiors have taken such an interest in this?'

Dominic stops mid-stride. He turns to address Gavin. 'That's because I don't know.' He smiles. 'I told you. This is beyond my pay grade.'

The lawyer opens the door, and as he leaves, Detective Inspector Carter rushes in. 'Chief, you're going to want to see this.'

• 37 •

THE FORGIVEN

Gavin, Jaydon, and several other major crime detectives watch the scenes of the riots unfold on the television pinned to the wall. They view the news mid-flow. 'The insurgence arose following the fatal shooting of one Justin Radford, a fourteen-year-old local.'

Fourteen, a child, Gavin thinks. Memories resurface. His thoughts shift to Devon.

Devon Maxwell was the nineteen-year-old he shot and killed as a uniform cop working the streets in Baltimore. His mother's name was Cecilia. A good natured, devout Christian. He knows this because he learnt about her, and eventually gathered up the courage to pay her a visit...

* * *

Gavin walked from his parked car to Mrs Maxwell's house with his heart in his mouth. It was a quiet summer afternoon in the neighbourhood. *He left me no choice...*

* * *

Gavin and his partner, Barry, lit up the berries and cherries on their black and white. They had spotted an erratic driver weaving along the city street.

The car slowed to a halt. They parked at a distance. Barry exited the vehicle and then approached the passenger side of the assailant's car. He did not get far before Devon jumped out of the vehicle and began spraying bullets from his Scorpion VZ61 sub-machine gun.

Barry was fortunate not to be shot. Gavin shouted several warnings during the intermission of gunfire that splintered the vehicle's door they sheltered behind, but to deaf ears.

It turned out Devon was off his psychiatric meds and hopped up on cocaine. Gavin took the shot, and Devon went down.

*. *. *.

He knocked on the door. Gavin glanced down at his clasped hands whilst he waited. His palms were sweating.

There was a sound of rustling bolts and latches. A woman in her mid-twenties opened the door. She crossed her arms and said no words, but if looks could kill.

Dee Dee called out, 'Mum,' whilst she kept her deadly gaze directed at Gavin. Cecilia Maxwell strolled to the door— a woman in her mid-fifties who had a calm demeanour.

'Mrs Maxwell, my name is–'

'I know who you are.'

Gavin found it nearly impossible to look this woman in the eyes. His heart raced as he trembled. It was also nearly impossible to continue speaking, but he did so.

'I tried. I tried everything I could. He just wouldn't stop. Determined to kill us both. I tried.' A single tear rolled down his face. He then looked upwards to find Cecilia's calm gaze.

She sighed. 'You see that red maple over there. When Devon was nine, he was obsessed with climbing that tree. My late husband told him not to, but he wouldn't listen. He eventually fell and broke his arm.

'Devon revelled in doing things he was told not to. That might be okay for some, but my boy was a troubled soul with a splintered mind.'

She enveloped her fingers around Gavin's clasped hands and held his gaze. 'I forgive you. Now it is time to forgive yourself.'

✳ ✳ ✳

'They need all available riot squad out there asap,' Gavin murmurs. His mind rests on the cop who shot the kid. *It's a hell of a thing to take someone's life.*

✳ ✳ ✳

Avery sits, braced against a wall, immobilised due to a broken leg courtesy of Chuckles and the mob. Owens holds the Heckler & Koch MP5 carbine firearm close.

* * *

A short while earlier, the mob descended on the officers. Owens fired a warning shot into the air that caused them to dissipate.

That's when he retrieved the additional sub-machine gun and a first aid kit from the vehicle mere moments before a shadowed hoodlum launched a fire bomb from the darkness—setting the car ablaze. Being armed with heavy weaponry had brought them some time.

* * *

Owens guards over Avery and the stabbed victim, who shivers but is still conscious. He dressed the man's wounds the best he could, and continues monitoring him. 'Are you okay, buddy?' Yasiel manages a nod of the head.

The two officers look over at the dead kid lying on the pavement. The mood is sombre. 'It was a righteous shoot.'

Avery ponders for a moment. 'I know.'

Immense heat radiates from the flaming vehicle as smoke rises to the sky. The distant wails of police, fire and ambulance sirens draw near.

• 38 •

ANGEL OR DEMON

Jaydon's mobile jangles a tune. The caller withholds their number, but it makes no difference. He knows who this is.

Jaydon takes the call after the second ring. Then, he composes himself before speaking. 'Doll face.'

'Very astute, Detective. I often wonder about those silly names the media comes up with. When did you figure it out?'

'Does it matter?'

Gavin monitors from a few yards away.

'Not really. So, you know what's next?'

'I guess I do.'

'It's time for me to set you free. Meet me at the abandoned industrial warehouse on the East Side in one hour. I've forwarded the address. Come alone.' There is a click, followed by silence.

Jaydon views the device in his hand like an alien object. Gavin is now at Jaydon's side. Jaydon rests his arm on his shoulder. He exhales deeply.

'What is it? What's wrong?' He locks eyes with his superior. His hands are shaking.

Jaydon removes a crumpled black-and-white photo of himself from his pocket. There is simply a question mark written in a red marker on the back of the photo.

Jaydon feels a sense of calm now that he is certain. He first suspected this had something to do with him when he visited the Colburn's home for the second time. 'I thought I was seeing things.' Jaydon recalls the night when he unravelled the first clue...

He came into contact with the word magnets that spelt, 'HELLO MR DOLL FASE,' on the Colburn's' fridge.

'As time went on. It became clear.' Jaydon revisits Mark's Summer's home in his mind...

He loomed over several photos on a nearby table. There was one particular picture that caught his eye.

The same photograph that is now in his possession. Jaydon moves forward. Gavin blocks his way. Jaydon's gaze is that of stone. 'I need to do this.'

The detective superintendent nods solemnly. 'I just wanted to give you this.' He hands Jaydon the firearm that was seized. Jaydon returns the temporary gun that he received. Gavin steps aside, allowing Jaydon to pass.

He watches Jaydon thoughtfully as he strides out of sight. 'Angel or demon.' Gavin then glances upwards at the rioters playing deadly havoc on the television pinned to the wall.

• 39 •

VALLEY OF THE DOLLS

Ilana's eyes open to the sound of clattering noise and the protest of the neighbour's dog from outside. She rises from her sleep into a sitting position. Her body is tense, and her breath quickens. Ilana gathers the courage to tread slowly towards her bedroom door.

Ilana is at the bottom of the staircase. Her bare feet touch the corridor floor. She stands in the moonlit corridor for a tense moment. A sinister shadow drifts past her window. She rushes to the kitchen.

Ilana opens the cupboard drawer and stumbles through cutlery and utensils to find a knife. She cautiously moves towards the living room. The pointed weapon held firm in her grasp.

There are more footsteps in the backyard, and another sinister shadow passes her window. Then, a bang on the door! 'Mrs Lynch, this is the police.'

Ilana pauses a moment to gather her thoughts. She then places the knife on a nearby table and finds the light switch. She moves along the corridor to the front door.

Through the peephole, she views a young patrolman. 'Show me some ID.'

The officer adheres to her request. Ilana presses a combination of numbers on the alarm keypad, then undoes the latch.

The policeman stands tall at the entrance. There is a marked vehicle with another officer parked a short distance away. He smiles reassuringly before speaking. 'I hope I didn't scare you, Mrs Lynch? I'm Officer Wilson. Your husband requested a watch on your home tonight.'

'Why? What's the matter?' Ilana asks with deep concern in her voice.

'I don't know for sure. They're causing havoc in The Slums, but the chief backed this.' Wilson hovers around the entrance awkwardly. 'So, we'll just be outside.'

Ilana looks him over from head to toe. She finds a warm smile. 'I'm sorry. Where are my manners? Would you and the other officer like a drink?'

'We wouldn't say no to a tea, ma'am, if it's not too much trouble.'

'No trouble at all. You boys come on in.'

On the drive to the industrial warehouse, Jaydon wonders how all of this will transpire. He knows there is a possibility he will kill this man. *What then?*

The detective briefly glances to his left. He spots The Slums in the far-off distance as he zooms by. There are traces of smoke and fire.

The killer formed an alliance with the psychiatrist. The psychiatrist also had help. *Was it from powerful people? Or just clever criminals?*

He puts that to the back of his mind. The only thing that matters is the immediate future. He is soon to come face to face with his daughter's killer. A man who remained one step ahead. A man who must have had connections to the investigation. This is the only thing that makes sense.

✻ ✻ ✻

Detective Jaydon Lynch exits his vehicle, weapon drawn. He pauses and breathes before making his way into the heart of darkness.

Jaydon moves through the industrial unit, which is currently going through a refurbish. This building was formally a mannequin factory. Slim, high cheek-boned, and ball-headed life-size models, which are uncannily human, are scattered within the factory.

There are also several mannequins shrouded in plastic sheets, presenting an opaque and translucent appearance. It's not lost on Jaydon what Doll Face is trying to do.

He moves past additional mannequins in a corner, about a dozen, thrown into a pile. Some absent heads and limbs. Their bodies twisted. Jaydon then spots a veiled shadow that weaves through the loose, flowing industrial plastic sheeting draped amongst metal scaffolding.

There is a sound of footsteps accompanied by a voice that echoes off the walls. A voice tinged with the local dialect. 'In a sense, this will be the first time we spoke since our phone call.' The voice changes mid-speech to something different, deeper, darker. King's English, but not quite. 'I no longer need to hide my true self. Neither will you.'

Jaydon's gun locks onto the voice. He moves forward. 'Come out!'

The shadow slowly emerges from the darkness. It's Detective Berg. Detective Berg is Doll Face. A cop moonlighting as a serial killer, or should we say a serial killer moonlighting as a cop?

'You don't seem to be surprised.'

'I'm not.'

'When did you figure it out?'

'Does it matter?'

I guess not. He spreads his arms wide. 'The best place to hide is in plain sight.'

• 40 •

CONFESSIONS OF A SERIAL KILLER

Perhaps it was Amelia's passing that triggered my impulses. Maybe I was born this way. I guess it doesn't matter now.

I, Callias Vasco Berg, am a serial killer.

Aged six, I had my first encounter with death—a goldfinch at the bottom of our garden. The bird lay on its side, yellow wings spread wide, and from the creature's off-red face, black eyes stared into nothing. There was purity, calm clarity, and truthfulness.

My father, Baron Jonathon Berg, was the owner of a well-known multinational confectionery company. He had inherited his noble title from my grandfather, but accumulated wealth mostly of his own accord.

He met my mother, Catalina, whilst on a business trip abroad. They married and soon were pregnant with twins— Amelia and I.

The Baron spent the majority of his time at the company. We hardly saw him. My mother was often emotionally unavailable. This did not matter because, as twins, we had each other. Even when we were not together, I never felt alone.

Amelia was socially awkward. When my mother sent her to boarding school at thirteen, things took a turn for the worse.

Some of the older girls made my twin sister's existence a living hell. Amelia became a facsimile of her former self. She was distant upon her return during the holidays, spending most of her time silently locked away in her room.

My mother saw the signs and made some effort in her own way, but it was not nearly enough. By the time they removed her, aged fifteen, it was already too late.

I climbed up to the roof on a winter afternoon after searching the entire manor. Amelia stood on its edge, captivated by whatever she saw down below. My sister turned, smiled, and then jumped.

At the funeral wake, some of Amelia's so-called friends offered their condolences. I knew by just looking at them. They were the tormenters. The leader, Elise Sutton, said, 'I am so sorry. We didn't expect this.' As she looked around to her sycophant friends for their support.

I said nothing. However, rage consumed me. There was then an uneasy silence, and the mood in the room shifted. Lead tormentor then hurried away, red-faced. Her sycophant friends trailed behind.

Fantasies began to emerge. Urges that were hard to keep at bay. I wanted more things to appear as the goldfinch did.

It started with insects, then larger animals, such as squirrels. The maid found our dead cat, Lilly, at the back garden gate.

I overheard my mother shouting at my father. 'He's just like Sterling, your brother. We have to do something.'

'We do, but I can't lose my son, too. When they find out what he is, they might take him away. I know people with access to resources.'

They said I needed help. If I was going to blend in, I had to mask what I really was.

They first introduced me to him when I was sixteen. He didn't go by the moniker of Cain then. I can't remember what he was called. He made me forget. There were a lot of things he made me forget.

By the time I was twenty, I had learnt how to fit in. I guess my good looks and superficial charm were enough of a disguise. All you need in this day and age is surface. My relationships during university did not last that long, but it didn't matter.

However, there was a resurfacing of a lingering urge. Not yet tangible. Opaque and just out of reach. Like a permeable shadow cloaked in a misty fog.

In my mid-twenties, I ran into Elise Sutton, my sister's tormentor. She now lived in the megalopolis. We had coffee at a trendy café bar.

She told me how guilty she felt about Amelia. She and her friends at the time were not the kindest at school. I listened, and something about her confession finally allowed me to remember. Right there and then, I knew I would kill her.

I projected false empathy. She became attached to me. Over time, it grew into a relationship. I am not sure if I had feelings for her. Though I told her that I did.

When the time was right, I made it look like a sleeping pill overdose with the use of clever shenanigans.

The detectives grilled me, but I was much smarter than them. They ruled it as an accident.

I did not divulge this information to him, but I disclosed my feelings during a session. 'The impulses I have. They are becoming stronger.'

He listened intently and, following a thoughtful pause, said, 'Your urges will soon become overwhelming. There is not much more I can do if you continue down this path. You need to have a plan.'

I returned to the stately home. One day, I climbed the ladder and entered the attic. I found a box with some of Amelia's old toys. What stood out to me was this strange doll. It looked so much like her.

Killing Elise was satisfying, but it didn't feel complete. Too much time had passed for her. I needed to take the lives of those who were becoming but had not yet crossed the line into a tormentor. Through me, they would maintain their innocence. Pure, like the goldfinch.

He devised a complete plan. I was to hide in plain sight by becoming a part of the very profession that I would evade.

Having an IQ of 155 and an unnaturally fit body, I could have sailed through the police recruitment process. The most challenging thing was to continue wearing the mask of someone with average intelligence.

Being a police officer was more pleasurable than expected. I found mixing with the low-life criminals of The Slums to be quite riveting.

We devised a plan for when I started. The cop on my tale would be one Jaydon Lynch, a man famous for catching people of my persuasion. I needed to get close. Graduating to a detective in Major Crimes was about as close as I could get.

The funds my father provided ensured I could move around with ease, whilst my profession provided vital information on how and what to avoid.

He instigated the plan brilliantly. However, throughout, I sensed resentment. I figured he was not helping me because he wanted to but via a forced hand. Was this through the request of my father's powerful friends? I wonder, *did*

he know what his son had become despite his intentions?
Did my mother still suspect?

Regardless, my fantasies developed into a reality that was as sublime as I imagined. I enclosed my fingers around their throats and watched the lights leave their eyes.

I have committed to my work, conserving innocence. Now, it is time for me to go the way of the goldfinch with the aid of Detective Jaydon Lynch.

• 41 •

EQUATION

What is an equation?

equation

noun

1. an equation is a mathematical statement that establishes quantities are equal through the use of numerical symbols

2. a problem in which several or many factors need to be well-thought-out

3. a situation in which you deliberate all parts of the complex whole for it to be understood

4. to create that which is equal or balanced

✳ ✳ ✳

Central Municipal Police Station staff are working at limited capacity due to the insurrections taking place. All riot-trained officers are now suited and booted in protective gear, trying to quell the disturbances that have erupted in a part of The Slums.

Cain stands near the door of his cell. 'Officer!'

Gilbert, the single Police Guard on duty, is watching the news live on a laptop. He momentarily tries to ignore Cain whilst monitoring current events as they unfold.

'I need to speak to you.'

Gilbert glances upwards. The officer rises from his seat and moves towards the captive's cell. He slides open the Judas gate and meets the eyes of Cain. Gilbert waits to hear the upcoming request from the prisoner, who says nothing. 'Well?'

Cain just offers an intense glare. 'Okay, I've had enough of this,' Gilbert says as he prepares to slide the Judas gate shut, but then Cain's voice immobilises him.

'Set me free.'

The voice is surreal, otherworldly, persuasive, commanding, and unnervingly calm. Now inside his head, becoming his own thoughts. Thoughts that he feels compelled to carry through.

* * *

Gilbert feels the cold concrete floor beneath him as he lies still. He blinks his eyes open to the tamper-resistant luminaries fixed to the ceiling that glow down upon him. *What the hell just happened?!*

He observes his surroundings and realises that he is in a prison cell. Cain has stripped him of his uniform, radio, and key card.

The officer is trying to figure out why he feels so afraid. He deliberates how much time has passed. Wanting to shout out, but something is stopping him.

*. *. *.

'You turned this whole place upside down, searching for me. All the while, I was right there under your nose.'

'With the help of Cain. Who else?'

Berg smiles darkly. He recollects what Cain asked of him. It was the same night he called Jaydon...

*. *. *.

'Are you willing to make the sacrifice?'

'What kind of sacrifice?'

'The ultimate kind.'

'Yes. Yes, I am.'

'Good. When you return home, I want you to make a phone call. Then you are going to find me some potentials.'

*. *. *.

Several weeks later, Cain sat in his office chair, cross-legged. He listened intently to a patient—one of many potentials.

'I don't normally do this kind of thing. Detective Berg recommended you. You see, I have these urges, violent tendencies.'

The man speaking was the firearms officer, Avery—Owen's partner, who shot the kid Justin.

Cain smiled, a smile that didn't quite reach his eyes. 'We'll see what we can do.'

*. *. *.

Returning to the night of the infamous phone call, Cain said, 'Then you lie low, and do nothing until the stage is set.'

*. *. *.

'Your clouded judgement stopped you from seeing me for who I really was. For who you really are.'

'Your sister—was any of that true?'

'Yes, someone took her life. From a particular point of view.' Approaching Jaydon, the serial killer utters, 'Now your eyes are truly open. The ending will be sublime.'

*. *. *.

Police Inspector Zinnerman enters the corridor; immediately noticing the empty area, he sighs.

'Constable Gilbert! How many times have I got to tell you? You can't go wandering off like that.'

Silence greets him. The Uniformed Inspector explores his surroundings and senses something is amiss. 'Gilbert?'

He cautiously moves down the corridor towards Cain's detainment cell. Upon reaching the detainment area, he is taken aback with shock and disbelief, exclaiming, 'Jesus!'

Through the Judas gate, he spots his fellow officer stripped of uniform, shrunk in a corner. An anxious mess, rocking back and forth, hugged into a ball.

Zinnerman reaches for his radio. 'I have an escaped prisoner and officer in distress. I repeat, escaped prisoner and officer in distress.' He opens the prison cell door and punches a nearby emergency alarm button with the side of his fist. The blaring siren pierces the air, notifying the entire building of an emergency, though it's too late.

*. *. *.

The looters behave as if it's a free-for-all day, rummaging through shops and setting cars and buildings ablaze. This causes ashes to fall from the sky, resembling snow in an old black and white samurai film.

They are located in this part of Kendersford, creating havoc whilst avoiding the riot police trying to deliver order a few blocks away.

A sole uniformed officer ignores the vandals and calmly continues on his merry way. However, he is not actually the police. Did he train as a psychiatrist? Who knows?

Curious to view the chaos in action and now amidst the unruliness. Cain thinks, *is this humanity at its most truthful?*

He wasn't completely honest with the detective. Yes, he opened the door for the potentials to walk through, but some were reluctant to move on their own accord. So he gave them a firm nudge. Why wouldn't he?

The Colburn lawyer was a scumbag who defended rapists and killers for a living. The less said about the billionaire CEO of the legal drug racket, the better. Yes, there were casualties, like the doctor, but he had to keep the detectives on their toes whilst making things interesting.

As for Callias Berg, Cain had just about had enough of watching him get away with those atrocities. All because daddy cosied up with the higher-ups.

That spoilt little monster called me a hypocrite. I guess I am. Regardless, if everything goes according to plan, the detective will put a bullet in his head, and that will be that.

Detective Jaydon Lynch turned out to be quite smart—a fascinating study. This may be the last experiment for the time being.

The Organisation has made it clear that things are to change in no uncertain terms. 'These experiments of yours must end. We can't afford to keep cleaning up the messes you leave behind. It's going to be hard enough to control the narrative of connected random murders goaded by telepathic hypnosis.'

The Colburn murder trial will just quietly fade away. Caitlyn will walk free. The Organisation will lean on the politicians, who will then apply pressure on the prosecution team. Settling the case away from media scrutiny is imperative.

The Organisation requires him to whisper in the ears of those close to the leader of the free world. He will play the role of an international diplomat. The current commander and chief seems to believe naively that he can decide things without their permission.

Cain walks through the crowd of rebels with no fear. They spot the cop but dare not approach. Why is that? What power does he possess? Instead, the insurgents part like the Red Sea, and he is Moses.

Cain disappears into the smoke-filled night, not to be seen again. Well, at least for now...

🐎 🐎 🐎

Berg stares right through Jaydon as he speaks. 'I am a gift to you.' He unclenches his fist and throws something at Jaydon's feet.

Jaydon slowly kneels to the floor and scoops up the item whilst keeping his eyes and gun pointed directly at the killer. He then rises and glances down at his hand to what is being held—an onyx stone necklace with an inscription of 'S' on its surface.

'I dumped her dead body thirty miles north of here in the woodlands.' Berg moves a few steps closer, iPhone in hand. His phone screen showcases a forest location marked with a pin. 'I've saved the coordinates for you.'

Jaydon glares at the scum with utter contempt. He moves closer, swiftly changes the gun to his other hand, and hits Berg with a phoenix eye punch to the sternum.

In Mantis Kung Fu, the practitioner focuses a concentration of force to the point of their protruding index finger, which is a staple of the martial art. When hit with this, it might feel similar to the pain of being stabbed without piercing the skin. Jaydon also elbows Berg and then pistol whips him in the head for good measure.

He stands above the killer, who lies winded and bruised. Jaydon thinks, *I am simply here to finish a job. Deliver death.*

'There was only one way this could end. What was I going to do, rot in a cell whilst becoming a tee-shirt of the week? No.

'This, however. They are going to write books about us. The serial killer police officer, who was a part of the investigation team for the murders he committed. Executed at the hands of the lead detective on the case for taking the life of his daughter. So beautiful, poetic, awe-inspiring.

'You're exactly like me. Playing the role of the lowly cop when you are so much more. I feel your pain. Your anger and frustration with the entire world. Now, we will both converge to make the perfect sum. An equation like no other.'

A large industrial fan embedded into the brick wall slowly spins. The luminance that disperses from an unknown exterior source causes a cyclical rhythm of shadow and light to fall across the detective's face.

Jaydon's hands shake violently. His palms tighten around the gun's handle. His fingers itch around the trigger. *Maybe the psychiatrist was right. Maybe this is all we are.* Suddenly, an impactful memory washes over him...

❋ ❋ ❋

He was driving down a secluded country road in the middle of nowhere, heading towards G-Pa's for a visit. His car broke down. It was cold and hammering down with rain. Jaydon placed his vehicle in neutral and steered it towards the muddy side of the lane.

As he waited patiently for the recovery vehicle, a woman in her early thirties slowed to a stop, fog lights glaring. She exited her vehicle and moved towards him in the dark of night, with only shadows of trees to be seen.

The young woman stooped over into view through the passenger side window. 'Are you okay?'

Jaydon glanced over at her car. In the back, he spotted a child sleeping soundly in an infant seat. No older than a year. The same age Sophia was during that time.

As a police officer. Jaydon felt the urge to lecture this woman for her own safety. As part of humanity, he felt a profound sense of love and connection. Jaydon held her gaze, smiled and calmy said, 'Thank you. I'm going to be just fine.'

✷ ✷ ✷

Berg closes his eyes, ready to accept his fate. 'I am a gift to you. A gift.' There is a long moment of silence...

He then feels cold metal being wrapped around his wrist. There is a sound of handcuffs fastening to a rail.

Berg opens his eyes to view Jaydon standing over him as he holsters his weapon. 'How many? How many mothers, brothers, sisters, and fathers that weep dry tears?

'You're going to help them find closure. I'm going to see to that.' He kneels and scoops up Berg's phone from the ground. 'Then you're going to spend the rest of your life rotting away in a prison void.'

Berg can offer no comeback, other than a bewildered blank stare. He then lowers his head in despair.

Jaydon leaves Berg handcuffed to the metal rail. He heads towards the sounds of distant police sirens. Jaydon Lynch moves out of darkness and into the light.

• 42 •

DEATH OF GOD

Detective Inspector Carter soars down the motorway to Wideforest woodlands. Detective Superintendent Gavin Reece sits in the passenger side seat contemplating.

The GPS signalling tracker he planted within Jaydon's gun immediately notified his phone once the weapon was drawn. He waited a while before sending out reinforcements. *As his superior, I should have stopped him, but as his friend. I couldn't.*

Gavin counted on the fact that there would be a resolution by the time the cavalry arrived. He trusted Jaydon would do what was just.

Upon ending the call with his DCI, he felt saddened by the finality of it all, but relieved that Jaydon chose not to kill Doll Face. *Would I have done the same?*

Gavin often wondered what he would do if it were him. His daughter Sage is all grown up and engaged to be married. A wonderful, stable, young woman. He could not imagine...

In the yoga philosophy, one is supposed to adhere to non-violence. Is that even possible? An officer dutifully ends the life of a mass shooter embroiled in a murderous rampage. *Is that violence?*

They won't have to search extensively, as Berg provided a location if he is to be believed. *Why would he lie?*

Gavin always felt something was off about Berg, but this. Over the course of almost three decades of policing, never has he seen anything like it.

What is almost as concerning was his superior's response. They seemed to be more anxious about the media blowback than the fact that a killer passed through screening, rose through the ranks, and murdered several young ladies whilst operating as a detective.

Gavin did not run a check on Berg personally, as Major Crimes Command is famous for its strict vetting process. *Berg must have been clean.* It will be interesting to see what information now comes to light.

His thoughts transition to Jaydon. *What will I find when I arrive?* The sign up ahead reads. 'Wideforest 10 miles'. DI Carter drives the pedal to the floor as they hasten towards their destination.

Rebecca Howard sits on one of the wooden chairs in the hospital chapel. This has recently been the doctors' mainstay during quiet periods. She still feels close to Isaiah here.

Dr Howard has never been devoutly religious. Her parents, both clinicians, remained agnostic, but always encouraged her to explore.

She gazes upwards to the miniature Christ, arms outspread, hands and feet nailed to the cross. Upon his head, which he tilts slightly to the right, is a crown of thorns. The light hovering down from up above, rendering him ethereal. Stain glass windows placed on either side, aid in creating the atmosphere of a compact place of worship. She recalls the end of one particularly tough day...

❋ ❋ ❋

Isaiah sat peacefully in this very chair. She took a seat beside him in silence. A few moments passed.

'Do you know what the cross represents?' He asked.

'He bore the weight of our sins, I guess.'

'The cross represents both the lowest and highest form of humanity. Those willing to torture a man to death are the most deprived, whilst Jesus symbolises the ideal. The pinnacle of what we should all strive towards.'

❋ ❋ ❋

Dr Howard considers the Nietzschean assertion that God is dead. *What would this mean if it were true?* There certainly is an argument for its validity.

Over several decades, we have made true advancements. Access to anyone in the world with the simple touch of a button. Yet, this generation is the most lonely, depressed, angst-ridden, and drug-dependent.

People no longer court. Instead, they swipe right for instant hook-ups. Others opt out of dating altogether. Communities are decaying, and birth rates are dropping.

We have abandoned the overarching story that grounds us in morality. Fundamental truths lay by the wayside. What has taken its place is an inferior, low-resolution tenet that has permeated art, culture, music, movies, and our general way of life.

Maybe the inspiration from Christianity, Buddhism, Hinduism, Judaism and other religions was actually an objective backbone that manifested in everything we held dear. *Isaiah, you have truly rubbed off on me.*

A voice draws her out of her thoughts. 'Doctor Howard,' Nurse Ashley says.

She turns.

'Sorry to interrupt. Several casualties are about to roll up. It looks like it's going to be a busy night.'

'Thank you, nurse. I'll be right there.' Her colleague departs.

Doctor Howard rises from her seat. She offers one more contemplative glance at the crucifix. Then heads towards the upcoming chaos.

• 43 •

BLIND NO MORE

Jaydon hurtles along the single-carriageway in an un-marked vehicle. The time on the car's dashboard reads *1:39 a.m.*

The lane markings of broken white lines are the only visible features amidst a seemingly endless road. Night surrounds the asphalt concrete, causing it to appear black. It reminds him of a Dorothea Lange photograph.

Why didn't I kill him? Was it an innate morality? Are the fruits of G-Pa's wisdom coming to bear? Was it something else? A misguided sense of belief? A cop that still sees the good in humanity. *Is that so rare?*

He recollects the heart-to-heart he had with the priest—specifically, the Buring Man ritual of the Hinutu tribe...

Father David held Jaydon's gaze. His eyes were the tran-quil blue of a calm ocean, with the same endlessness.

'The victim's family has a choice: to either save the killer or let them die a horrible death, suffocating in intense heat.

'The Hinutu believe if they let them die, the aggrieved have their revenge. Though the victim remains in the after-life, blind and alone, waiting for someone to guide the way.

'However, if they save the culprit and show mercy, the victim regains sight, and the family can move on with their lives.'

*. *. *.

Jaydon focuses on the empty road ahead. He contemplates where it is about to lead.

*. *. *.

Jaydon Lynch slows to a stop near the woodlands upon spotting DSI Gavin Reece and DI Carter up ahead. His col-leagues trod sombrely towards the vehicle.

*. *. *.

Rays from their flashlights beam through the shadowy for-est as Jaydon, Gavin, and Carter hike towards their destina-tion. The GPS map informs them they are close. Gavin places a hand on Jaydon's shoulder as they proceed through the wooded hills.

* * *

Sunlight breaks through the cloud, casting a diffused glow. The birds, who have chosen not to migrate, chirp a melody to accompany the ambience of nature's wake-up call. Ilana sits in her studio, where the radio delivers news that plays low in the background.

The Newsreader says, 'As the violence escalates, there is no end in sight for the continuing anarchy. A lengthy enquiry will surely take place regarding what some are already predicting to be one of the worst riots in years...'

Earlier, she received a call from Jaydon. He said little, apart from being close to confirming Sophia's whereabouts.

Ilana has known for a while that her daughter has long departed. What troubles her is the feeling that Sophia is not yet ready for her next life.

The Newsreader gains her attention. He says, 'Following being stabbed several times, reports state that the community leader, Yasiel Caddel, is in stable condition at City Hospital.

'John Avery and Finn Owens, the original firearm officers on the scene, are providing a detailed report on what transpired, leading up to the current events.'

The artist gazes distantly into what was once a blank canvas. Combining the hard, abstract, multicoloured strokes has resulted in the formation of a dragonfly. Wings buzzing in still pose.

Ilana hears her husband's muffled voice conversing with the young officers, piercing through the walls. She senses darkness looming, but still chooses to rise from her seat and head towards it.

She wanders into the corridor, where Jaydon stands silently. His shoes are muddy, his clothing filthy. Ilana keeps her distance.

'Where's Officer Wilson?'

'I sent him home.'

Ilana spots the necklace in Jaydon's grasp. It's hand-made, natural onyx stone with 'S' inscribed on its surface.

Ilana's fingers unconsciously move towards her lips, palms pressed together. Her eyes hold Jaydon's. She then nods to herself.

Jaydon slowly moves forward, his arms outstretched. He reaches Ilana just as she collapses to the floor.

The sound of Ilana's wailing is pure heartbreak, the epitome of human emotion at its most sorrowful. Over her shoulder, Jaydon sees Sophia standing, watching. The wailing of her mother takes precedence. Her tears dampen Jaydon's back as he comforts her.

The one thing he notices before his daughter drifts away for the last time is her expression. She is calm and at peace. Blind no more.

• EPILOGUE •

It's close to daybreak. Sunrays dance amongst the sky, painting the blue clouds with oranges and pinks. Darkness has lifted.

Jaydon Lynch finds himself captivated by the beauty of this wonderful beach. As for the ocean, one could easily lose themselves in the enormity of liquid aqua—an infinite number of droplets moving in perfect unison to form the ocean's vibrational pull.

Jaydon's hair has grown out. The white linen clothing he wears lies comfortably on his skin. He carries a look of health and vitality.

Jaydon senses a presence on his back. He turns slowly to find his wife and offers a smile.

✻ ✻ ✻

Ilana strolls towards her husband. She wears loose-fitting, light-coloured summer wear and sandals and is carrying a green urn. Her presence is that of calm.

There was significant concern that Sophia's passing would be one of anguish. Yet, the night Jaydon broke the news, she experienced an unexplainable sensation. Somehow, she knew her daughter would be okay.

One day, her child's soul will return as part of a new family. This might be several years from now or many. Whenever it occurs, it will be a rebirth with good karma.

Ilana slows to a stop at her husband's side and admires the breathtaking view. Something is very different about her appearance. The loose clothing does very little to hide the fact that she holds a child.

She was selfish in her grief, closing off from everyone. With this new birth, she wishes to share the joy with both of their families. Though Jaydon only has his grandmother left.

Ilana opens up the urn. Ashes sprinkle up and away into the sea breeze. Jaydon holds her close whilst lightly caressing her tummy. He remains stoic.

A single tear trickles down her cheek. A tear forged from deep sadness and a renewed joy.

ACKNOWLEDGEMENTS

I cannot express enough thanks to my sister Sonia for her enthusiasm for this initial concept, and continued support from gestation to realisation. You have always been an encourager of ideas, fanning sparks into flames of creativity.

When *Equation* was initially a film project, my producer, Hannah North's dedication and work ethic, were second to none. Thank you so much for your hard work and unwavering belief.

I also express my gratitude to acting legend Sir Derek Jacobi for his keen interest and kind words of encouragement many years ago. Though the film did not quite come together. The project has manifested in another form.

Amongst the countless research that I conducted in writing this book, the following article was paramount:
Yingxu Wang, PhD, P.Eng, F.WIF, F.ICIC, SMIEEE, SMACM (2007). Cognitive Processes of Human Perception with Emotions, Motivations, and Attitudes, *International Journal of Cognitive Informatics and Natural Intelligence* 1(4):1-13

HUBERT-RICHARD CLARKE

Hubert-Richard Clarke, is a filmmaker, actor, musician, martial artist, yogi and writer. When not teaching yoga, or practicing Kung Fu. He will most likely be studying philosophical scriptures, learning piano pieces on his old Korg Trinity, or enmeshed in one creative endeavour or another.

If not in Birmingham, you might find Hubert-Richard in Bali guiding Yogis. He was one of the first in the West Midlands to achieve a high-level black sash grade in Southern Mantis Steel Wire Kung Fu, which was a great honour. Hubert-Richard has a Film-Making and Creative Digital Media degree from the University of Worcester. *Equation* is his first novel.

Milton Keynes UK
Ingram Content Group UK Ltd.
UKHW041748161124
451235UK00004B/265

9 781068 651526